TRAVELING CLOTHES

BILL DEASY

velluminous

Published by Velluminous Press
www.velluminous.com

ISBN: 978-1-905605-18-7

COVER DESIGN
HOLLY OLLIVANDER

TRAVELING CLOTHES

for Paula

Beverly Moon walks slowly along Allegheny Avenue. The January cold doesn't bother her today. She knows she'll be leaving it soon, together with all the other drab details of her sad Fairmont life: Abraham, Jessica, Imperial's – the thick, heavy grayness surrounding her like a gauzy blanket.

In her mind she chooses her outfit. She sees the matching black dress, stockings and panties laid out in a row on their bed. She sees herself putting them on, looking sexy and bold as she walks quietly away and breaks free once and for all.

For this last night she won't let on, she'll play the role she's perfected over the past several years: a woman resigned to her fate … a woman who just doesn't care any more. Jessica will already be in bed. Abraham will give Beverly space as she fixes herself dinner, gets undressed, then falls to sleep beside him after mumbled goodnights – all for the last time.

They'll think she had a choice. They'll think she should have just made the best of things – for his sake and for the sake of their little girl. What they won't know is that if she had stayed, she would surely have killed him, or died trying.

One more day – then everything changes.

1

Will drives. The Allegheny River runs parallel to them, but in the opposite direction. It offers Claire Jordan neither comfort nor quiet answers. Once they've crossed the bridge, turned right into town and reached her apartment above the little card shop, she finds it is no longer the safe haven she had so painstakingly created. The beige walls adorned with prints of Van Gogh and Monet, the bookshelves overflowing with meaningful trinkets and sacred texts, her '67 Gibson acoustic resting on the hand-me-down brown couch–all seem like the signs of some stranger's life. Not hers. Not this sad Friday morning.

"Can I get you anything?" she hears him ask as she climbs into bed. She doesn't answer. He joins her there and cradles her firmly from behind.

"Why do I feel so terrible, Will?" she asks, crying again. "We weren't ready for this anyway."

She turns over and looks at him.

"I don't know, Claire. I'm sure so much of it's physical. Your body's been through a lot."

She senses his dissatisfaction with his own words, his unqualified diagnosis. Even in her pain, she wants to reach out to him and tell him it's all right to think out loud with her and that nothing he says will be the wrong thing, so long as he says something. She doesn't mind how much she needs him at that moment.

They sleep. She awakens hours later and feels him beside her. Once she is sure it wasn't a dream, the finality of the change hits her again. She hears his gentle snoring, briefly considers being offended by it, but lets the temptation pass.

She remembers the night last August when they first met. She played her "Joe's-Place" debut – an audition of sorts, though Joe assured her he was a generous judge of talent. A Tuesday, the crowd was slim to start and by the time her set wound down, could hardly be called a crowd at all: the daffy, blonde waitress whose un-amplified speaking voice easily rivaled Claire's microphoned singing one; three barstool drinkers who kept their hunched backs to Claire for her entire fifty-minute set; Joe, the friendly owner who watched at first then disappeared into a back room; and the handsome-as-hell young bartender, Will, who was the only one paying attention. Claire used the courage she possessed only when making music to meet his eyes as she sang.

They talked afterward, the night becoming a marathon conversation as they boldly threw flesh and blood onto the skeletons of their life stories. Claire smiled as she described her home life in the sprawling bland suburb of Pittsburgh called Penn Hills.

"My two big brothers are just plain crazy," she laughed. "I felt like I was growing up in the middle of a kickboxing match. Somehow, in the middle of all their wild boy chaos, my mom realized I could sing a little."

"You have an amazing voice," Will interjected.

"My dad had a friend who played guitar and he gave me some lessons," Claire continued. "I pretty much lived for music from that point on. My mom and dad were so great about supporting me with all that, whatever I happened to get into. They drove me to play auditions and band rehearsals and all the concerts I wanted to see."

"My mom was like that, too," Will said. "Super-supportive. My dad died when I was a baby, and my mom was like a superhero trying to give me a happy childhood. Anything I showed even the slightest sign of being into, she'd knock herself out encouraging me to do. I realized pretty early that for me my thing was writing," he continued, smiling sheepishly as he ran his fingers through his short black hair. "It's kind of weird, really. I mean, I think I knew since I was about four that I wanted to make up stories and write books all my life. I want to have my first novel finished by the time I turn twenty-five."

"How old are you now?" she asked.

"Twenty-three."

"And have you started it yet?"

"Not so much," he admitted.

"Well you better get cracking, dude."

As they talked into the night, they discovered that their tastes and views were like different colors on the same rainbow, they just went together somehow. His love of Ryan Adams seemed to complement her obsession with Patty Griffin. Her love of Shakespeare somehow balanced out his worship of Hemmingway. They assembled their details like pieces of the same puzzle.

Life's randomness was a good thing, they agreed, as she explained her impulsive decision to blow off graduate school and accept the surprise offer from Ira Mendelson, her English professor at the University of Pittsburgh. She came to work for him at the quaint little bookstore he and his wife owned in the sleepy hamlet of Fairmont, Pennsylvania.

"So, you came here to write songs, and I came here to write stories. Words and music, Claire, we're words and music."

"Did you just quote Eddie and the Cruisers?"

She remembers how blissfully aware she was of his hand on her back as he guided her to his giant old Plymouth. They drove Fairmont's quiet streets for hours continuing their back and forth rambling. The morning found them parked by the Catholic Church–huddled and shivering in the front seat, still talking as the sun bled slow daylight overhead.

She wonders what their baby would have looked like.

Claire doesn't leave the apartment all weekend. Will only does to rent movies from Video Corner and to pick up the dinner he ordered from Angelo's. Claire strums her guitar but can't bring herself to sing. There are fleeting moments when she almost forgets what has happened, what she has lost.

"Do you think the two of us will ever have children together?" she asks him late, late Saturday night.

"Yeah, Claire, I do," he replies, and his answer gives her comfort.

Fairmont is a half-mile by half-mile square that rises up from the river. Twenty-seven miles from downtown Pittsburgh, it sprang up in the late 1800s around the thriving Edgewater Iron Works. Though that industry has weakened in recent decades, the town thrives still, a tourist attraction for easy-to-please city dwellers hungry for simplicity. Every year, some new trapping is voted in by the town council to maintain the old-time feeling: a useless wooden train shelter on the exact spot where one stood a hundred years ago, a granite rendering of the Iwo Jima flag raising, a white clock tower across from the post office. In the past five years, a small band of artists and musicians has infiltrated the community. Bookstores and funky cafés are slowly replacing the family markets and beauty salons.

Railroad tracks separate the twin main boulevards. Allegheny Avenue, the cobblestone, favorite son, boasts the better shops and restaurants and is closer to the coveted mansions on the hill. Freeport, the tar-paved black sheep, is slightly more ragged in appearance and is reserved for the massive eighteen-wheelers that regularly pass through town. The streets that lie parallel with these are numbered, beginning with First just above the river, and ending with Twelfth at the top of the hill. State streets run perpendicularly.

Families have been here since the town's foundation passing down homes, stories and secrets from generation to generation.

To many, still, traveling to Pittsburgh is as preposterous as driving to New York or Los Angeles or some other faraway metropolis. Townsfolk are content to patronize their favorite local taverns Saturday night, and the crowded corner churches Sunday morning, just as they did last weekend and the weekend before.

Sunday afternoon Will surveys this quaint kingdom as he leaves Claire's apartment and begins the short walk up to his place on Sixth Street. In a flagrantly uncharacteristic move, he impulsively steps into an empty church he was passing. Though Will has managed to avoid organized religion all his life he suddenly craves the atmosphere he imagines exists in places of worship. Taking a seat in the back, he notices Jesus looking down at him from the massive crucifix above the altar. The quiet in the church and the stillness surrounding the troubling image seem to magnify the dying man's frozen agony.

Will is surprised by the tears that he cries then. In his heart, he was relieved by Claire's miscarriage. Though he maintained a brave, happy front since receiving the news of her pregnancy two weeks ago, his insides were definitely not aligned with his outsides. He was scared, no two ways about it, and reluctant to move away from his planned life course so early. Writing was all he wanted to think about, not a child, not a wife, not yet.

The pew is uncomfortable. How do people sit in these things an hour at a time, Sunday after Sunday he wonders? What are they doing when they come here? Are they seeking something they haven't found, or yelling out their answer? Why is he mourning the loss of a life he was in no way prepared to welcome?

He kneels and decides the kneeler is no better than the pew. His elbows fall on the wooden divider in front of him. His fingers fold in front of his face. To an observer, he would appear to be praying. Maybe he is, he decides. Maybe he's kneeling here praying for the woman he loves and the child they'll never know.

Twenty minutes later Will walks into his apartment. The heat hits him like a brick wall. It's only the beginning of June, low seventies and breezy outside, but his one-porthole attic hideaway feels like a Taiwanese sweatshop. A broken-down air-conditioning unit leans against the wall to his left. The only items of furniture on the unfinished wooden floor are a dresser, cot, and oversized desk and chair. His prized possession, the battered Smith Corona his mom gave him for his fourteenth birthday, sits atop the worn oak.

He dropped out of the University of Michigan and hit the road three years ago. The classroom couldn't hold his attention. He needed to live, to travel, to experience. He'd pumped gas in New Jersey, cut grass in Ohio, and jumped at the chance to follow a smiling Joe Camden back to Fairmont from the Amnesty International Concert they'd both attended in D.C. How better to learn about life and accumulate stories that would fuel his fiction for years to come, than by tending bar in a small town? And though he works most days at "Joe's Place" and sleeps most nights at Claire's, he manages to spend at least twenty hours a week up here writing in his steamy sanctuary. He's only succeeded in squeezing out a handful of short stories, and his weekly column for the *Riverside Reporter*, but he knows he's getting closer to the story that he'll burn to tell.

"Hi, Cat," calls Lindsay from the bottom of the stairs as Will emerges from his room. She and her mother live on the old house's second floor. Until six months ago, Will thought Lindsay was the quietest kid he'd ever seen. Then one day, they happened to be leaving the house at the same time and Will bought her a chocolate parfait from the Good Humor Man. Lindsay the icicle became Lindsay the free-flowing river of affection.

"Hey, Mouse. How's your day going?"

"Bor-ing," she sings in reply.

"Where's your mom?"

"Inside, with Phil." She opens her mouth and inserts her right index finger as if to induce vomiting.

"Is he really that bad, Lin?" Will whispers, chuckling a little.

"He treats me like I'm a kid."

"You are a kid."

"You know what I mean. Can we shoot basketball tomorrow before you go to work?" She has his schedule memorized. Sometimes when he's writing she comes upstairs and alerts him to his pending tardiness.

"Okay. But you're not going to beat me at H-O-R-S-E again," Will declares. "I'm bringing my A game. You're going down."

"No, you're going down!"

"No, you're going down! How's twelve o'clock sound?"

"Can Claire come?" Lindsay asks. Though Lindsay likes Will, she worships Claire, even going so far as to copy Claire's shoulder-length hairstyle.

"She's working. We're coming to your T-ball game on Tuesday, though," he adds. "How have you been sleeping, Lin?"

A few months back, Lindsay's mom confided that her only child had been having nightmares, all centering around global catastrophe. Will chalked it up to Mrs. Ramsay's CNN addiction. Sometimes, Lindsay goes weeks without a good night's sleep. Will asks her about it whenever he notices dark circles appearing around her sparkling, blue-green eyes.

"Not so great," she answers.

"Have you been doing what I told you?" he asks. He'd given her a crash course in some basic relaxation techniques.

"I forgot," she admits.

"I'll give you a refresher course tomorrow, Lin. Don't take yourself so seriously. Try to remember you're seven." He extends his right fist and she hammers it gently with hers.

"The Pirates are not committed to the future." This is not a tentative, open-to-discussion opinion. It is a statement of fact, a decree from Fairmont's leading baseball philosopher, Larry Paul. He issues it from his customary stool, and taps loudly on the bar with his chubby right index finger. He needs a refill. "All they care about is staying in the black. No one in the ownership has any vision."

Joe shakes his head and retorts, "I disagree, Larry. I think they have the nucleus there for something special." He grabs the empty glass from the counter and fills it from a tap. "Maybe not next year, but the year after that, they'll win the division. We just need to be patient."

Joe has an uncanny ability to mix earnestness and sarcasm. It doesn't help that his appearance is somewhat comical: balding in the front; long, curly, Cowardly Lion hair down the back; a thick blonde mustache that blocks his nasal passages so that he always sounds congested. And yet, as he points out at least once a week, he's "curiously handsome." His Pirates prediction inspires groans from the audience.

"We've been patient for the past seventeen years," Larry barks, clearly offended by Joe's naiveté.

Bartholomew Tucker, the world-renowned painter who moved to Fairmont after retiring from his post as head of Carnegie Mellon's art department, smiles at the banter. He now fills the role of colorful art-genius–a role that stood vacant since Fairmont's inception. Having been shielded from sports all his life, he can't seem to get enough of these meandering deliberations.

"Patience is a virtue," he imparts, not minding in the least that he's universally ignored.

"What the hell are you talking about, Joe?" asks an amused Dominic Perchetti. "'Get a load of this guy," he urges no one in particular. "What do you know about baseball? You're what, thirty-five? Your father, now he knows baseball."

Joe's dad surrendered the bar to his eldest son six years ago. The walls are decorated in two separate and distinct styles: Pittsburgh Pirates memorabilia supplied by Joe, Sr., and autographed band posters provided by his son.

"Well, my dad's down in Florida, Dom. And I'm thirty-seven, by the way," Joe states defensively.

"Ah, you're too busy planning all your music trips to know anything about baseball," Larry asserts, referring to Joe's annual tradition of making a long drive–"spiritual pilgrimages" as he calls them–with his brother, Stanley, to see one of his stable of favorite artists. The next one's coming up in July: Neil Young at Madison Square Garden

"Music feeds my soul," Joe declares. "Sue me."

Larry spots Will and says, "Tell him, Will. The Bucs committed to sucking or what?"

"Definitely, Larry," Will replies in his confident barroom sports voice. Since his mid-teens, people have mistaken him for an athlete. His tall, lean frame and short, jet-black hair give him the appearance of a guy who might have played AAA ball, someone whose knee might have blown out, cutting his promising career short. Of course, nothing could be further from the truth. But Will lets the misconception stand. He wouldn't want to disappoint the peanut gallery. It's all a part of his research.

"Tell me about it, stud," purrs Donna, the chesty, bleach-blonde waitress, quoting "Grease," which Will recently, regrettably, admitted to watching one too many times. At the moment, there are no diners in the "dining room"–that area separated from the bar by a pair of pool tables–so Donna is free to play solitaire and flirt with Will, her two favorite hobbies. Though her age falls somewhere on the northern side of thirty, Donna's attitude and outlook remain firmly fixed in adolescence.

"Hey, Donna," Will answers.

"Where were you all weekend?"

"Claire's grandfather died," he lies. "We had to go to Altoona."

"We missed you," she coos, impervious to what he said and the commitment it implies.

"Watch the bar, Donna," Joe instructs as he extricates himself from the baseball summit. "Can I talk to you in the kitchen, Will?"

He lifts the wood divider at the end of the oval-shaped bar and indicates with a shrug for Will to lead the way.

"How's Claire?" he asks as soon as they reach their well-lit destination among the suspended metal pots, pans, and cooking utensils.

Will continues to be impressed by Joe's compassion, not only for the people in his life but for those oppressed and suffering around the world. Many weekend nights he puts on acoustic benefit concerts for political prisoners or disaster survivors. He happily loses customers who would rather go down the road to Duke's where they can drink in peace to the jukebox song stylings of Hank Williams Jr. and Mariah Carey.

"She's all right. Thanks for giving me the weekend off."

Will had called Joe from the hospital on Friday and told him about the miscarriage.

"Don't mention it, man. Tricia and I had the same thing happen a while ago. That stuff can mess with your head. How are you doing?"

"I'm good. It was just tough watching Claire go through all that. It's pretty intense."

"But she's all right?" Joe asks again.

"She's all right, I think. It's just gonna take a little while for her to feel like her old self."

"Should I get someone else for the gig Friday?"

"I'm not sure, Joe. I guess just assume she'll do it unless you hear otherwise. Could you do me a favor, though? Don't say anything to her about all this. She doesn't know that I told you."

"No problem, man."

The two friends emerge from the kitchen to find Joe's long-time girlfriend, Tricia Poe, sitting among the pundits. Her eyes meet Will's and her head's slight nod indicates knowledge of his and Claire's weekend ordeal.

"You okay, sweetie?" she asks as Will sets her standard vodka and orange juice on the bar beside her hands.

"Yeah," Will answers. "Thanks."

"Is Claire okay?" she follows softly enough so that only Will can hear.

"She'll be okay," he assures, leaning closer.

"That's the stuff you'll churn into your writing, Will," she observes. "I know that might sound calloused, but it's true. Pain is a killer teacher."

Will notices that Tricia seems "made up," the shade of her lipstick matching that of her eyelids and her sweater, all of it maximizing the blueness of her eyes.

"What are you up to today?" Will asks. "You look nice."

"Same old, same old," she replies, smiling from his compliment.

The two commence to navigate the familiar terrain they have claimed for their own–writing and philosophy. A shared love of Richard Russo had cemented their bond in the cultural wasteland that was Fairmont. Between random refills and occasional interruptions from the regulars, they talk easily for the next half hour.

"Literature 101 needs to conclude now," Joe says amiably as a new group of patrons enters the bar. "I need Professor Will to help me serve my customers."

"I was just leaving anyway," Tricia says, standing. Joe leans across the bar to kiss his girlfriend hello and goodbye in one fell swoop.

Will's thoughts are never far from Claire. He calls her every hour and takes a Joe-approved dinner break to run her some soup from the kitchen. On the way there, he stops outside the post office and plucks a flower from the modest garden at the base of the flagpole. She's sleeping when he gets to her apartment so he leaves the simple care package on the kitchen counter along with a note saying he loves her.

It's 2:30 a.m. The bar's been closed since midnight. Joe's boom box is perched atop a table playing Bruce Springsteen's *Darkness on the Edge of Town*. Joe, Will and Donna are finishing off the fifth of Cuervo Gold they cracked two hours before–three shots to go … one apiece.

"To Nelson Mandela," Joe says reverently.

"To Nelson Mandela," repeat Will and Donna, their elbows touching as they lick the salt from their hands then lift their glasses.

"Who's Nelson Mandela?" asks Donna, whose voice has grown more piercing throughout the late-night drinking session.

Joe looks at her, appears to be about to speak then thinks better of it.

"That does it for me," he slurs, stumbling to his CD player and thwacking the stop button. "I gotta get home. Tricia's gonna be pissed."

"Who's Nelson Mandela?" Donna repeats, a fraction of a decibel louder than the first time, directing her inquiry to Will this time, who quietly suppresses the gag reflex that followed his last slug.

"Pirates' new shortstop," he replies.

"Want to come to my place, Willy Boy?" she blares. "Hey, Willy Boy, want to come to my place?"

She's leaning into him. Her mouth is less than an inch from his ear. He can feel her breath on his neck.

"What's at your place?" he asks.

"You'll have to see to find out. Pretty deep, huh, Willy Boy? 'You'll have to see to find out.'"

With that, she stands, and attempts to lift Will from behind.

"Whoa! What the hell are you doing, Donna?"

"I just thought you needed a lift," she explains and becomes wildly amused with her pun. "Walk me home, sailor?"

"What the hell," Will replies.

"See you tomorrow, Joe," they yell in fluky unison.

Donna yells "Jinx!" as they support each other through the front door.

Tricia sits in her idling car with eyes fixed on the bar's front door. When Joe was late getting in, she knew he'd initiated his monthly Cuervo Summit. He was pretty predictable, really. Always on Sundays. Always on days she stopped by the bar. He'd come home three hours later than expected, stumbling and smelling like Mexican cactus juice.

It's Will she is waiting to see, though. She knows he'll come out first, and she likes the fantasy of herself running across the road to him, intercepting him, leading him to her car, to her arms, to her bed. No, to his bed. Seeing him in person makes the images more tangible, even though in reality, it will be her signal to get her ass home.

She can pinpoint the exact moment she fell in love with him. It was the second time they'd spoken – at the bar, on a slow Sunday not unlike the one this afternoon. She was amazed by the speed with which they'd bypassed superficialities and cut straight to the deep stuff. Pain. Sadness. Meaning. In the only compliment she could manage at the time she'd told him that talking with him was like talking to herself, they were so similarly wired, so eerily connected. She wonders for at least the thousandth time if he felt it too.

There's the door. To Tricia's surprise and disappointment Will is not alone as he exits. He's attached to Donna. Fucking Donna. Happy-go-Lucky, Good-Times Donna. That whore. Clearly they're both drunk. Clearly Will doesn't know what he's doing.

As Tricia races home, she works the infuriating sight from a negative development to a positive one. Will is making a drunken mistake. He's human. The door is open, though – the door she'd been sure was closed due to his relationship with Claire. For whatever reason, Will is vulnerable right now. That is a good thing.

The 500 block of Twelfth Street boasts the best available view of the town and the river below. Unsuitable for development because of the gas line maze that runs beneath it, it has become, through the years, the prime make out location for local teens.

At 3 a.m. on a Monday morning, Joe has the unofficial overlook all to himself. He'd transferred *Darkness on the Edge of Town* from the bar to his car and, as he listens, feels certain that through some trick of cosmic connection, the Boss was channeling Joe's future frame of mind when he laid down the vocal for *Racing in the Street.* There's a resignation there, in Bruce's trembling narrative, that resonates with Joe, albeit drunkenly.

He pictures Tricia and Will that afternoon, speaking like she and Joe never did, never had. And who was she kidding getting all dolled up like that to see the young bartender? The whole thing makes his heart feel heavy. Why can't love be easy, he wonders?

He needs another pilgrimage. He needs to get the hell out of Dodge for a few days. He'll pull out his traveling clothes and hit the highway again–this time for the Big Apple to see Uncle Neil with old faithful Crazy Horse. Joe would get a break from Tricia, from everybody, and really be himself–just him and his little brother, Stanley.

He smiles through the mist of fading consciousness, remembering last year how happy Stanley had been when Joe started their adventure by making a surprise stop at the FBI headquarters in downtown Pittsburgh. A friend of their father's was the director of operations and treated them like royalty, serving them coffee and donuts before taking them on a tour of the place. Stanley, whose mental deficiencies had kept him childlike even in adulthood, and who had always fancied himself an amateur law-enforcement official, laughed with giddiness as they tried on bulletproof vests and held the "Tommy Guns" Al Capone's boys had used back in the days of Prohibition. Joe recalls it all as he puts the car in reverse. He thinks about Stanley. Poor Stanley was up to his old tricks again. They'd have to have another talk soon.

Joe hits the repeat arrow on the dashboard radio. In what he believes to be pitch-perfect unison, he sings along with the top of the song and begins the slow drive home.

The tips of Donna's large breasts graze Will's sternum.

"Could your T-shirt be any tighter?" he asks.

They're in her apartment. He can't remember walking over.

"Maybe I should just take it off." Before he can respond she follows her own advice and removes the cotton garment. "How's that, Willy Boy?"

He wants more than anything for her to stop calling him that but is distracted by her cleavage and the pretty white lace of her bra, which barely conceals its bountiful contents.

"The bra looks a little tight, too," he says. "That's not a criticism or anything. It's just an observation."

She bursts out laughing as she takes his hand and guides him to her bed.

🍂

Monday morning Joe Camden, Sr., sits on the porch of his unit at Vistana, the upscale condominium complex in Orlando, Florida that he's called home since leaving Fairmont six years ago. He drinks decaffeinated tea and thinks about the day ahead.

He'll start with his hour-long walk along the narrow sidewalks that bisect and outline the dozens of constructed lakes and streams dominating the forced tranquil landscape here. The thin, tinny voices of sports experts will whine through the small headphones of his portable satellite radio as he stops to feed the greedy ducks, pretending they're happy to see him. He'll take a leisurely mid-morning swim then lie by the pool reading a mystery book for an hour before returning to his unit for lunch and a hot shower. This afternoon he'll check out the Pirates game. It might even be televised since they're playing the Marlins. The big decision after that will be, "to Bingo or not to Bingo?" He'll probably take the plunge. Too much solitude can drive him batty.

And yet, solitude is exactly what he wants—at least in a general day-to-day way. Since Martha died six years ago he hasn't sought a new companion, or even a friend, though he does miss his time with the boys at the bar back home. He smiles as he pictures them all there debating life's finer points and verbally crucifying the sports coach of the moment.

Joe Camden, Sr., sits alone in the shade of his enclosed terrace, observing the minimal signs of life outside: a passing landscaper, a bird in flight, leaves moving slightly with a breeze. He thinks about the day ahead so he doesn't have to look behind at the faint, small, insignificant trail he's left in the course of his seventy-seven years on this earth. Were he to turn and peer back, though, his eyes would surely see the missteps. One, in particular, would stand out.

🌿

Sunlight falls across Claire's face and gently awakens her. It's there again, the stone black emptiness. With every ounce of energy, she forces her legs over the side of the bed, her feet onto the cool, wooden floor.

It's her first shower since Thursday. She shaves her legs, washes and conditions her hair. She wipes the steam from the mirror that hangs beneath the wall nozzle and studies her drawn, dimpled face. Her brown hair, black with moisture, still falls to her shoulders. Her clear skin remains freckled and fair, her brown eyes specked with green. But something is gone.

As she dries and dresses, she wonders why Will never came. He'd left his car with the tacit understanding that he'd be back after work. He always slept over on Sundays. Oh well. The muse must have called.

The Mystery Lover's Bookstore is two doors down from the Hallmark Shop. Claire's proximity to her workplace is a double-edged sword. She can't easily avoid the Mendelsons' random crisis calls, but it's nice being able to sleep in, especially on the mornings after gigs.

It's 9:50 a.m. She unlocks the door, hits the light, walks behind the coffee counter and brews up some house blend. It will be an hour at least before she sees a customer. She throws in a Patty Griffin CD and skips straight to *Burgundy Shoes.* She swears the song, and the singer's rich, soulful voice singing it, conveys all of life's joys and sorrows, the whole confounding tapestry. The telephone startles her. She picks it up on the second ring.

"Mystery Lover's Bookstore."

"Claire, it's Finbar."

"Hi, Fin."

"I just wanted to make sure you remembered tonight," he says. "I have to leave here around six. Load in's at six-thirty."

It had completely slipped her mind. Finbar's band had a benefit concert in Pittsburgh and she had agreed to babysit Makenna. She has a moment of terror. Spending an evening with a seven-month-old baby does not exactly sound very appealing in her delicate state.

"I'll be there at six," she replies, cursing her own self-pity. Finbar, after all, has a far greater claim on grief. His wife, Maggie, died giving birth to the baby girl Claire promised to watch. Finbar, she knows, is just barely holding it together.

"Are you sure?" he stammers. "I could ask my folks if you forgot."

"No, I remembered. I can do it," she quickly replies through the growing lump in her throat. She hangs up the phone and stares down at the black-and-white checkerboard floor.

Tricia is nervous. She's been nervous all morning. It was all she could do to keep track of the crisp bills she disbursed from First National's drive-thru window. She sits in her Toyota Camry, checking her make-up, composing herself. It's 11:15 a.m.; she took an early lunch.

She looks at his mailbox and smiles at the uneven, gold-stenciled lettering: WILL JAMESON. She glances at her reflection in the window to her left and wishes she'd changed into blue jeans, curses the space between her front teeth, detests the fake streaks of red in her black hair, wishes she was prettier.

The front door, the door that all three tenants share, is open. She lets herself in and walks the two flights of stairs up to his apartment. Her heartbeat quickens with anticipation. She's imagined this moment for months, since they started having their talks at the bar.

"Will," she says, too softly to be heard. "Will," she repeats, louder, as she knocks on the wooden door with the upside down "3" on it. "Hey, Will, it's Tricia, Tricia Poe. Are you there?"

She's both relieved and terrified when she hears his footsteps approaching.

"Hi, Tricia. What's up?"

He's dressed in faded blue sweats and a red T-shirt. He looks pale but good. He always looks good. He holds a towel in his right hand. His hair's wet. If he's surprised to see her there, he doesn't show it. She takes this as a good sign.

"I'm really sorry to bother you, Will. I was wondering if we could talk." She is aware of her skin and of her body beneath her clothes. She is aware of the catch in her breathing. "I just needed to talk to someone."

"Have a seat," he says, pointing at the cot. "Sorry the place is such a dump." He pulls the chair out from his massive, old desk, just the kind of desk she'd imagined, and sits down across from her. "What's up?"

"I'm not really sure where to start," she says softly, deeply. She's been told that her voice is sexy and she wants to use it to full effect. "Are you sure this is an all right time?"

"It's fine, Tricia. I don't have to be at work until two."

"Are you and Claire doing okay?" she asks. Though the question would seem to be about the miscarriage, she is hoping he might take it more generally and seize the opportunity to open up to her. She flashes on the image of Will and Donna stumbling arm in arm the night before.

"We're great," he responds with more conviction than she'd expected. She wonders if maybe he'd come to his senses before giving in to his coworker's dubious charms. The thought creates conflicting reactions of relief and disappointment. Maybe he wasn't so vulnerable after all. "So what's up, Tricia?" he asks again. "Is this about Joe?"

"Yeah, it is," she admits. "And you have to promise me you won't tell him I came here. He'd kill me."

Will nods.

"Here's the thing, Will." She pauses, hesitating. "Joe isn't who everyone thinks he is." She studies his reaction to this—her planned opening statement. He doubts her already. She can see it in his eyes. She soldiers on. "I know that you and everyone else in town see Joe as this lovable teddy bear who wants to save the world. But there's a lot of stuff nobody knows. Pretty weird stuff."

"Like what?" Will asks.

She forces herself to wait before speaking, carefully choosing her words.

"It's okay, Tricia," Will reassures. "Pretend I'm a priest."

"Well, I found a bunch of bizarre movies beneath a floorboard in our bedroom closet," she says, feeling herself passing the point of no return. "And I mean really bizarre, Will. I'm no prude, but these were like dark, dark films. The girls in them were being raped and hurt and they couldn't have been near 18. I mean, they weren't little kids, but they weren't adults either. It was just twisted. I could barely look at them."

"Did you ask Joe about it?"

"Of course I did," she answers. "I showed him the movies and asked him what the hell he was doing with them. He said they must have been there when he bought the place."

"Well, maybe that's true," Will says.

Of course he'd side with Joe. They were practically best friends. Joe was the big brother Will never had.

"There's more though, Will," she continues. "He makes me feel like shit. And if I ever even look at another guy he freaks."

Will looks at the floor, then the wall. He sighs as his eyes finally reconnect with hers.

"What about me?" he reasons. "You and I talk all the time. He doesn't seem to mind that."

"He does, though, Will. At first he didn't, but lately, when I mention your name or talk to you at the bar he gives me the evil eye and lets me have it later. No one ever sees that. I feel so alone. I'm thousands of miles from home. I've pretty much lost touch with my family. I don't have any real friends here. And everyone thinks Joe's a fucking saint. You're the only one I can talk to."

She tries desperately to lure sympathy out from behind his blank expression. She feels like this is her only chance. She doesn't know what she'll do if Will doesn't understand, if he doesn't believe her.

"Why don't you just leave him, Tricia?" Will suggests. "If what you're saying is true, why don't you get the hell out of there?"

"I don't know, Will. I'm too afraid of what he'd do. He's really mean. I know that's hard for you to believe, but it's true. If I left he says he'd find me and…"

She breaks down crying. At this point in her wild imaginings Will had come to her, held her in his arms, spoken kind words, made love to her with passion and creativity. But this was not a fantasy. Will sits speechless, no closer to her than when she began. They are interrupted by a loud thump on the door.

"Will," a child's voice calls. "It's twelve. Ready to go?"

"Oh shit," Will exclaims, and looks at Tricia sheepishly. "I promised my neighbor I'd shoot basketball with her. Wait a minute, Lin," he yells. "I'll tell her we'll play later."

He stands and starts for the door but Tricia stops him, saying, "That's all right. You go." She was crazy to think Will would shift his allegiance so easily. "I shouldn't have laid this on you anyway. I'll figure something out."

"Tricia, really," he says. "We'll talk more later. Maybe it's not as bleak as you think. Just give me some time to think about what you're saying."

"That's all right, Will. I'll be all right. I'll see you around."

She rushes from the room feeling more alone than ever.

🌰

Abraham hates Mondays. It takes so much effort to reemerge, week after week, from the dark hole of his one-story house and face the world that gave him up long ago. Though he has not had a call or received a customer all day, the energy expended is still considerable. He sits behind the counter, a neatly organized rack of every kind of key imaginable shimmering behind him, and reads the latest *Outdoor Life* for the third time.

He opened the shop a little less than twenty years ago, right after everything happened. He'd had a nest egg, a surprise windfall from his mom's expedient cancer, and he used it to pay off the house in Fairmont and create this unprofitable, weekday getaway in Sharpsburg, just across the river.

Abraham Moon, Locksmith

He had the words, a boldfaced lie, printed on the front door, and learned from a book the basic skills necessary to perform the infrequent jobs he attracted. He can hardly remember his days manning the forge at the Iron Works, the job he'd taken straight out of high school and worked until his world fell apart.

He makes it a point never to close up even a minute before the appointed hour. It's all about routines. It's all about rituals. Finally, the little hand hits the five, the big hand hits the twelve and he permits himself to stand, stretch, hit the lights and leave. He starts the giant, yellow El Dorado he's owned for years and listens to the KDKA news as he drives two miles up Sandstrom and turns right onto the bridge.

Joe and the tall kid are behind the bar talking with the usual array of early evening drinkers. As Abraham retreats to his corner table, he overhears someone say, "He's got to learn to keep his dick in his pants."

A glass of whiskey and soda appears before him. He'd been looking out the window and doesn't know who set it there. Probably Joe Camden–the only one in this town who doesn't treat him like a leper.

Abraham withdraws, not into his thoughts but into his absence of thoughts, the quiet he has constructed between his ears and behind his eyes. He has mastered the art of not thinking. As he takes a sip and looks around, he has, literally, nothing on his mind. He simply sees things: the loud blonde waitress arriving for her shift; Joe pulling his long hair back into a ponytail as he referees the afternoon's debate; chubby Larry angrily arguing his point as mild-mannered Dominic smiles and shakes his head in passive rebuttal; Tom Larkin and Chuck Proffer–men he has known all his life–the easily amused spectators drinking in the harmless, hollow, comical tension; the new guy, Bartholomew the painter, limping in and taking the bar's last empty seat.

Jessica arrives like a monsoon, ferocious and unexpected. All eyes turn to the doorway where she stands, tall, dark and beautiful, looking for him. Finally she spots him and approaches. She is seething.

"I told you I needed the car," she spits. "You promised me you'd come right home."

She doesn't say, "Dad." She never does. And of course she wouldn't understand about the importance of his rituals. Of course she didn't know it was impossible for him not to stop for his whiskey and soda, no matter what he'd promised. He feels the weight of the old, familiar stares that say, "You are pathetic. You are a waste of man." He feels the men ogling his absurdly beautiful daughter, his only child.

"Give me the keys," she says.

Why is she so mean? Didn't he sacrifice everything for her? Didn't he give her clothes, four walls, an education? He stands slowly.

"Drive me home," he replies in the cool, calm monotone he knows she finds infuriating. She grunts her irritation and storms out the door ahead of him.

"You can put your tongue back in your mouth," Donna taunts after the mystery woman leaves the bar.

It's the first thing she has said to Will since starting her shift ten minutes before, and he takes it to mean that it's business as usual between the two of them, in spite of last night's drunken episode. He had awakened before dawn, fully clothed, horrified by the sight of her semi-clad body, uncertain of what had transpired, and left in a cloud of self-loathing.

"What was that all about?" Will asks the patronage at large. "Who was she?"

"Jessica Moon," Dominic volunteers. "Abraham's daughter."

"I've never seen her before," Will says. He would definitely have remembered.

"She just moved back from Nashville," Joe explains, clearly sharing his friend's wonderment. "Where'd she go to school again, Dom?"

"Vanderbilt," answers Larry, who adds, "She's a looker, that one. I'd like to bend her over my Rolodex."

"I think she wanted you, Lar," Joe says sarcastically.

Joe likes to tease Larry whose weight, somewhere in the neighborhood of two-hundred-and-fifty pounds, and hyper-productive sweat glands hinder his success with the ladies, though he still talks a good game, always, for some reason, utilizing imaginary office props.

"Did anyone notice the way she checked out Larry?"

"What's Abraham's deal?" Will wonders aloud. Though he's seen the man almost every weeknight for nearly two years, poured and served him countless drinks, before this evening, he'd never heard him speak. He was just the tall, quiet guy who always sat at the same corner table.

"You never told him about Abraham, Dom?"

As the resident Fairmont historian, Dom is expected to provide all newcomers with the essential town legends. A seven-year widower and retired postal worker, he normally relishes the role. Tonight he is reluctant.

"I don't know, Joe. I don't think we need to be digging that one up."

"Come on, Dom," urges Larry. "Tell the kid the story."

Dominic sits quietly for a moment. The deep lines that surround his eyes fold into one severe crease as he squints back through time. The effort looks painful.

"It happened on a Friday night in January nearly twenty years ago," he finally begins. "Abraham had a fight with his wife, Beverly. Some neighbors overheard them. Three days later, he reported her missing."

The gray-haired elder statesman stops unexpectedly. Normally generous with details, he seems to have said all he cares to on the subject of Abraham and Beverly Moon.

"Jesus, Dom," Joe says. "What kind of storyteller are you?" Joe picks up the baton and starts running. "When Abraham went to the police he was all scratched up. And when they searched his house that Monday, they found Beverly's license and keys–stuff you'd think she'd take if she was leaving; especially the license. Abraham became the only suspect. But they could never find any evidence."

"He always said he was innocent," Larry adds. "And some people believed him. Not many, but some. Thought she just hit the breaking point and left. Some people even said they heard her talk about it. But most of us thought he did it."

"What about the daughter?" Will asks. "Didn't she see anything?"

"She was just a little kid," Larry replies. "And she was staying at her grandma's if I'm remembering it right."

"So what do you guys think?" Will follows. "You think he did it?"

"Yeah," Larry says without hesitation. "I think she was about to leave him for another man, and he killed her in a jealous rage. A friend of mine says he knew Abraham in high school and that he was a real gun nut. Says the minute he heard about Beverly disappearing, he knew Abraham did it. He said Abraham always scared him even though he never talked. Or maybe it was because he never talked."

"Abraham's smarter than he looks," Chuck Proffer, a committed waffler, volunteers in support of both sides.

"Yeah, and he's handsome, too," Donna interjects. "What?" she adds when faced with a look of unanimous annoyance. "He's a hottie. Ever seen his eyes?"

"I don't know," Joe interrupts, ignoring the grinning waitress. "I've always liked Abraham. He's a good guy. He used to take my dad hunting all the time. My dad thought Abraham was some kind of hunting savant or something."

"Further proof he could kill someone and no one would ever be the wiser," Larry interjects.

"He just doesn't seem like a killer," Joe continues. "He doesn't have a killer's eyes."

"Not all killers look like Charlie Manson," Larry suggests, as the age-old debate resumes.

Will listens, enthralled, happy to have stumbled upon such a fascinating story. He spends the rest of the night asking questions.

Dominic leaves early.

2

Stanley Camden kept to himself. Joe, his big brother, said it was best that way. Joe always seemed to know what was best.

In one month's time they'll be setting out on another one of their pilgrimages. They'll pack up Joe's car with food and beer and listen to music as they travel to whichever cheap motel Joe has selected as their home base – always somewhere close to the concert venue.

They met Will Jameson on a pilgrimage to Washington. They became instant friends, the three of them. Will met them back in Fairmont a week later and became Joe's new bartender. Life was funny like that. Life was funny in a lot of ways.

Stanley parks across from the bar and sips his milk. He thinks about Washington and Woodstock and Nashville and Athens. He thinks about all those years and all those trips.

"We need quality brother time," Joe says. "It gives me a chance to hear what's on your mind. Make sure you're doing okay."

They talk and they drive and they laugh. Once a year. Fifteen years now.

Pilgrimages.

Just before midnight Claire hears Dan Finbar's footsteps ascending the stairs to his second floor apartment. Had he arrived fifteen minutes ago, he would have found Claire standing beside his sleeping child's crib, weeping quietly. But now she is recovered and sits on the living room couch watching Letterman.

"Hi, Claire," Finbar whispers after setting his guitar in the kitchen. "How was she?"

"Perfect," Claire answers as she finds the remote and clicks off the television. "She didn't cry once. She just crawled around all night, smiling at everything. I don't think I've ever seen a happier baby."

"She eat all right?" he asks.

"A whole jar of squash and then a bottle of formula before she fell asleep."

He looks into the room where his daughter sleeps, returns to the living room and sits on the couch with Claire.

"How was the show?"

"Pretty good," he replies.

He looks the same as he has every time she's seen him since Maggie's death: tired. His eyes, his body, exude physical and spiritual fatigue. His smile is only a fraction of what it was that day a year ago at the bookstore when he asked for a recommendation and she turned him on to Dennis Lehane. Once they realized they both played guitar and wrote songs, their fate as friends was sealed.

"It's hard to play," he says. "I still associate it so much with Maggie. I didn't realize how many songs she inspired. I have to force myself not to think too much when I'm singing. It's tough."

Though Claire had not known Maggie well, she had liked her very much. With Fin on the road much of the time, Maggie would pass an occasional hour talking and laughing with Claire in the bookstore café. Claire had witnessed firsthand the light that grew brighter with each month of Maggie's pregnancy. She could only imagine the pain Finbar carried.

"Are you doing okay, Claire?" Finbar asks. "You seem a little down tonight."

"I had a tough weekend, Fin."

"You want to talk about it?" he asks.

"I had a miscarriage Friday," she blurts as her expression shifts from calm to crushed. "I'm sorry," she says, embarrassed as she starts to cry.

She falls into him, and he holds her. Grief resonates between them like a tuning fork.

"I'm so sorry," he whispers. "I'm so sorry, Claire. You should have said something. I could have found another babysitter."

"I don't know why I'm so upset about it," she stammers. "If you asked me a week ago if I wanted this baby, I probably would have said no. I'm just so sad, Fin. I don't know why I can't stop feeling sad. Looking at Makenna, it's hitting me that I lost a real baby, my first child. And I feel so ashamed for not wanting it. I'm afraid the baby knew."

Holding her upper arms, Finbar gently pushes Claire away and seeks out her eyes with his.

"Claire, you didn't cause this to happen. And whatever you think you thought, it had nothing to do with the miscarriage. That's just not how it works." He squeezes her arms for emphasis. "You'll have children, Claire, when the time's right. When you're really ready. And you'll be a great mom. And you'll learn something from the pain and the strangeness you're feeling now. I promise."

Muffled words interrupt, crackling through the baby monitor; Joe Camden's distinct voice breaking through the distortion. "Sorry," Finbar says. "It picks up his cordless phone, sometimes." Joe is Finbar's landlord and next-door neighbor. Finbar shuts off the monitor as Joe drones instruction to someone, probably Will.

"How's Will handling everything?" he asks. "Has he been there for you?"

"Yeah," Claire answers with her first smile in days. "He's been a real trooper."

Finbar sits in the living room darkness. He looks out the window at a trio of telephone lines. These are the times when it's hardest, right after somebody leaves and the sound of voices is replaced, again, with silence. These are the times he misses Maggie most.

Just eight months ago she was here with him still. After friends left, as Claire just did, they would straighten up together, hand wash the dishes in the kitchen sink, add their private final comments to the evening's group discussion. He might pause as he walked behind her to wrap her in his arms, rest his hands on Makenna, still hidden but kicking her "hello."

There are no dishes to wash tonight. There is no discussion to finish. Maggie is gone. He feels none of the gratitude or grace he described to his sad friend just an hour before. He sits and he waits to grow tired.

When Makenna cries, Finbar is glad for the distraction. He goes to her and whispers that it's okay, daddy's here. He rocks her in her mother's favorite chair and softly sings her mother's favorite song. How sad, he thinks, that this perfect little girl will never hear her mother's voice or feel the warmth and comfort of her mother's embrace.

And yet, as Makenna's eyes surrender finally to sleep, Finbar remembers again why it's a good thing that he's still on this earth.

The Monday crowd had been bigger than usual. Donna sweeps the popcorn and napkin littered floor and hums the theme from *Grey's Anatomy,* a television show she swears holds all of life's answers. Will lifts the barstools and sets them upside down on the bar. The place has been closed ten minutes and neither of them has said a word.

Will can't shake the feeling that something has been lost. Just as he knows that he should tell Claire what happened–that he got drunk and passed out in another woman's bed–he also knows that he won't.

"Want to have another slumber party?" Donna asks.

Will despises her at that moment. He wishes he could remember exactly what they did. It couldn't have been much. It probably wasn't anything.

"No thanks, Donna," he replies, trying to sound casual. "I'm heading over to Claire's."

He means this as a not-so-subtle hint, and a statement of his unwavering loyalty to the woman he loves. As usual, Donna seems to edit Claire's name from his words.

"Rain check, then," she says, unaffected, smiling confidently.

Later, Will stands out on Allegheny Avenue. He walks the quiet cobblestone blocks. The promise of summer hangs in the warm breeze. He sits on the post office steps and gazes at the mountainous skyline, a jagged black jigsaw beneath the June moon. He tells himself again that he has nothing to feel bad about. He'd had a stressful couple of weeks. He got drunk. Chances are, nothing happened.

By the time Claire gets home Will is showered and in bed. The lights are still on, and he's lying awake. As Claire enters the room he is overtaken by a fresh wave of guilt. He's certain she will see it in his eyes. She walks over and sits on the mattress, even with his chest, like a mother by her little boy, then completes the image by leaning down and kissing him on the forehead. She still looks sad.

"What was that for?" he asks.

"I love you," she says.

"I love you, too." He reaches up and touches her hair, then traces a trail down the side of her cheek. "How are you doing?"

He can't believe he hasn't spoken to her all day.

"A little better," she replies. "I had a nice talk with Finbar. He helped put things in perspective a little."

Will feels a twinge of jealousy. A twinge he would not have felt before last night.

"I thought you'd cancel," he says. "Wasn't it hard babysitting?"

"Yeah," Claire confesses. "But just think about what Finbar's going through." She tosses her T-shirt on the floor, reaches back and unclasps her bra. Will wonders when they'll have sex again. "Where were you last night?" she asks.

"I ended up getting drunk with Joe and staggering back to my place," he half-lies, adding, "sorry," and secretly applying it to all he hasn't said–a version of the finger cross.

"That's all right," she assures him. "I think I actually needed the time alone."

Claire performs her nightly rituals and Will recounts the Moon saga first and then his bizarre afternoon conversation with Tricia Poe.

"Luckily Lindsay saved me," he concludes. "I really didn't know what Tricia expected me to say to her."

"She expected you to say, 'I'm madly in love with you, Tricia. I'll save you from the evil Joe,'" Claire teases, hitting the lights and joining Will under the sheets. "She's in love with you, Will. I could have told you that six months ago."

"But what do you make of what she said about Joe?" he asks, brushing aside the love allegation. "Do you think she was telling the truth?"

"No, I don't," she replies. "I think she'd say pretty much any-thing to get into your pants." Will is still surprised sometimes by the combination of sweetness and earthiness that defines Claire. She squeezes him once from behind to indicate that sleep time has arrived and they could revisit the matter in the morning. "'Night, Will."

He flips over and kisses her once on each closed eye.

"'Night, Claire."

Will can't sleep. Rather than continuing to brood over the previous night's tragic error in judgment, he guides his flooding thoughts to Abraham Moon sitting at his corner table, expressionless before his daughter's bitter barrage. Will wonders what secrets the broken man harbors. He sits up as quietly as possible then climbs out of bed and puts on his clothes. The note he leaves Claire reads, "Gone to write. See you tonight. Love Will." He knows she won't mind. She never does.

Whenever there's a choice between walking and driving somewhere, Will chooses the former. Walking is one of his greatest writing tools. It's then, alone, often at odd hours, that ideas flow most easily. On this night, he listens to Pete Yorn on his iPod and enjoys the sensation that his life is a music video—it puts him in a cinematic state of mind.

Though all the streets in Fairmont are similar, each has its own particular flavor. Washington, the street Will walks now, is the "hidden business" street. Though it looks like just another string of homes, several of the buildings are actually small family enterprises: Tepe Chiropractics, Donnelly and Sons Law Firm, Smith's Antiques.

Passing the humble, camouflaged companies Will ponders Claire's assessment of the Tricia situation. On some level, he knows that Claire is right and that Tricia harbors some feelings for him, but he'd assumed those feelings to be harmless and small. Maybe he had been wrong.

He remembers a girl at the University of Michigan who berated him for being so clueless when it came to women. After a year of happening to be in the majority of his classes and dropping by his dorm room to bring him coffee two or three times a week, she confessed the burning crush to which he had, in fact, been oblivious. Maybe he was clueless.

An approaching car turns its headlights to high, momentarily blinding Will. Joe's familiar voice yells out, "Hey, Will, what are you doing out so late? Don't you know Fairmont is a breeding ground for dangerous lunatics?"

"Hey, Joe," Will says, happy for the sudden company, feeling, somehow, that the chance encounter is proof of Joe's innocence–not that Will needed any. "I was just thinking about you."

"You know I don't swing that way, right?" Joe asks gravely.

"You don't?" Will replies. For a fleeting second, he considers mentioning the visit from Tricia but decides against it.

"You need a ride?"

"No," Will answers. "I'm just thinking about doing some late-night writing."

"Good luck with that then," Joe says as his car begins inching away. "See you tomorrow, brother."

Will resumes walking. He reflects upon the town of Fairmont and the way, upon his arrival here, he instantly felt an ownership over it—as if each tree, each house, each friendly face was his to use however he saw fit, assimilating each vivid detail into the wide-open world of his fiction.

He thinks also about secrets, his and everybody else's. "You're only as sick as your secrets," he remembers overhearing not long ago. He'd written the line down, thinking he could use it in something. He notes the fact that it was a sickening feeling withholding the truth from Claire, harboring a secret from her.

Donna. Tricia. Abraham Moon.

Secrets.

The *Riverside Reporter* is a small-time operation if ever there was one. Hank Shaw, the town's only real-estate agent, runs the paper from the back room of Fairmont Realty. It is his prideand joy.

Will planned on stopping by the office the next morning to pound out the column that's been percolating in his head but decides that there is no time like the present. Hank gave him a key after he read Will's first article and told Will to feel free to come in and use the computer whenever he felt the urge. So far, Will has only felt the urge on the mornings before deadline. He's always worked best under pressure.

As always, the place smells musty. It's all metal and wood: wood desk, metal typewriter, wood counter, metal service bell, wood wall paneling, metal filing cabinets. The prevalence of these two basic elements, along with the black linoleum floor, gives the room a harsh, dated, 1950s feel. Will passes an assortment of framed, vacuous slogans Hank seems to live by ("Slow and Steady Wins The Race," "To Thine Own Self Be True…") and opens the door to the back office.

The newspaper, a weekly, four-page offering of local events, homespun recipes and gardening advice, was taken over twenty-three years ago by Hank Shaw, who regards his operation as a vital cog in the vast machinery that is journalism. And for all its flaws, it is a treasured community possession. Will was stunned by the feedback he received after his first article appeared. Everywhere he went someone had something to say about it.

Will sits at the desk. On a whim, he does a web search for Abraham Moon which produces only one item—a short article from the Associated Press in which the basic details of the disappearance were reported. Will jots down some notes, then stares at the blank word document on the computer screen. Finally, the sentences come:

How does hearsay become legend? What turns rumor into lasting, local lore? What secrets lurk in the heart of any small town? What secrets lurk in the hearts of us all?

"Joe's Neighborhood Bar" is as good a place as any to find the answer to these questions. You never know what buried skeleton might show up on a given night. This past evening, for example, a story was related to me of events that took place long ago. And though it seems like dark legend, I'll leave it for you to decide.

Beverly and Abraham met in Riverview High School when they were teens. After graduation, they married and Abraham got a job with the Edgewater Iron Works. Beverly found work at a local dry cleaner. It was there, in the tiny shop on Maryland, she was last seen leaving work almost twenty years ago.

January 26, 1989…a Friday. The sky was threatening snow. An unforgiving wind blew in off the river. The sounds emanating from the Moon household were nothing new to the late-day stragglers hurrying home after work. A woman's ferocious shouting. Crashing glass. An object of furniture falling to the floor. Typical behavior from the unhappy couple within. Only this night was different, for it led, in one way or another, to the disappearance of Beverly Moon. Three days later, on Monday, January 29, Abraham reported his wife missing.

According to him, she'd left in a fit of anger late that Friday night and not said where she was going. According to him, his wife, whom he suspected was having an affair, waited for this weekend, when their small daughter would be sleeping at her grandmother's, to abandon them. According to him, his face was scratched as a result of his attempts to keep his wife from venturing out into the blustery night.

It was not long before Abraham became the primary suspect and focus of the investigation. To this day, no one knows to what extent his skills with guns and hunting might have helped him to commit the perfect crime. No evidence was ever discovered incriminating him in any way.

I'll leave you with a few final questions. Did Beverly Moon simply leave her husband and six-year-old daughter? Did she walk out the door into the frozen winter night never to return, or were darker forces at work? When does a rumor become lasting, local lore? Maybe, when it's true.

Too many A&E documentaries, Will thinks. Of course, he could never print it. Joe would probably ban him from the bar for life, possibly even run him out of town. Joe liked Abraham and wouldn't want his young employee dragging the sad man through the dirt again.

He returns his attention to the screen and proceeds to churn out his real column for the week. Using the computer mouse, he slides the unprintable Moon piece into the WORKS IN PROGRESS folder he keeps on the computer desktop and e-mails the editorial to Hank.

White, brown, black, green, tan, dark blue, light blue. Hank Shaw's top dresser drawer contains seven stacks of cotton briefs, a color for each day of the week. White is Sunday, the Lord's day.

Tuesday morning he slips on his trusty blacks and revels, as always, in the utter snugness, the total containment. He dresses for the important day ahead (D-Day: the day he assembles the week's stories and molds them into a living, breathing piece of print media) and attacks his circled lips with breath after willful breath whistling a Frank Sinatra medley, the Nelson Riddle years.

He grabs his newsman hat, the stylish gray Fedora he wears only on Tuesdays, only on D-Days, from the hat rack just beside the mirror that holds the picture of his mother. That picture is the last thing he sees before he leaves the house each morning. Her image, frozen in Kodak eternity, contrasting with his animated, smiling, red-cheeked, present-day face, reminds him anew of how deeply he loved the woman. On these days, D-Days, he knows how proud of him she would be. He smiles at her and resumes his maniacal chortling.

Hank's secretary greets him, as she does every morning: "Good morning, Mr. Shaw. Coffee?"

As always, Hank replies, "Good morning, Irene. Yes, please!"

Hank cherishes (privately, of course) their wordless efficiency and relishes each instance of Irene knowing exactly what he will do or say. They are a team, a well-oiled machine, and have been for seventeen years. She hands him his mug filled to just below the rim–two sugars, light cream–as he passes her station on his way to the back office.

"What have we here?" he thinks as he opens his e-mail. "Will must have been burning the midnight oil." He reads the essay and smiles at the boy's obvious gift, a natural writer. One day, Hank knows, his young protégé will go on to bigger and better things but hopes Will won't feel like his time with the *Reporter* was wasted. There's no substitute for experience Hank likes to say.

Will's WORKS IN PROGRESS folder sits tantalizing Hank, who does not resist the temptation to click it open. He always rationalizes these invasions of privacy by telling himself that he needs to monitor his charge's progress, make sure Will doesn't stray from the pre-appointed path. Hank is stunned by what he finds there.

"How the heck did Will get a hold of this one?" he wonders aloud.

When the story first broke in the winter of '89, Hank had been all over it. He released "Special Editions" four days in a row and devoted his front page to the disappearance for nine straight weeks. Reading Will's provocative little piece reminds him of those glory days, when the town seemed to revolve around the publication of his newspaper, and his articles, his musings, were the talk of every restaurant and barber shop. He places Will's intended story in the folder and moves the Moon article into the "drawing board" file. He's already convinced himself it was Will's mistake, not his. It had been late. Will was tired. He sent Hank the wrong story. That's already how Hank remembers it.

Look at him, she thinks. Look at how hard he works. Look at how focused and serious he is. Look at that poor, lonely man.

Seventeen years. That's how long Irene Turtleman has been working at Fairmont Realty. Seventeen years. Slowly the layers have fallen away and she's come to see him, to see Mr. Shaw, for who he really is, and not for the hard-nosed journalist he pretends to be.

Dr. Phil says the children we were are always inside of us, walking around with us, dictating much of what our grown-up selves do, feel, think and say. Well, she can see that the child Mr. Shaw was had never been properly taught how to love. And it makes her love him all the more.

Dr. Phil also says that pathologically shy people such as herself need to overcome their fears by taking baby steps. A series of baby steps, he assures, can eventually accomplish the same result as one big step. So, she's been trying to do the small things, like looking Mr. Shaw in the eye when she says hello and walking back and saying goodnight before she leaves each evening. All baby steps. All progress. "Slow and Steady Wins the Race."

"Yes, Mr. Shaw, right away," she tweets back to him, adjusting her hair then grabbing the requested file and walking it back to his office.

He hates it when she does this. She lies in bed. She won't say anything. He doesn't know what she wants him to do.

"I gotta go, Trish."

Nothing.

"Trish," Joe tries again, "I'm taking off."

Not a word.

"If you love me, don't say anything." In the past, a more comical approach has sometimes done the trick. Not this morning.

"I love you, too," he says. "I'll see you tonight."

The Prince of Fairmont. That's what Dominic calls him. Joe Senior is the King, and Joe is the crown prince. Joe has to admit that he knows pretty much everybody in the small town. He can't drive ten yards without waving to someone.

"You better get over to the bakery, Dan," he shouts to the traffic cop standing by the stop sign. "I think someone else is eating a donut."

"Hey, Joey," Dan shouts back. "Can't you tell I'm on a diet? I lost three pounds this month."

"You are looking awfully svelte," Joe comments as he inches his car forward. "Coming to the show this weekend?"

Joe is relentless in his promotion of benefit concerts. This week's is for the Pittsburgh Soup Kitchen.

"Not sure," Dan replies. "Have to get the hall pass."

"Get your house in order, man," Joe says. "See you Friday."

It's a brilliant, sunny day. The sky is a cloudless, electric blue. Joe throws in the latest Bob Dylan and is instantly soothed by the timeless sound. How does the old bird do it, he wonders? This is one of the poet's all-time best, in Joe's humble opinion–a future classic.

Singing along, Joe admires the painting on the wall at the end of the main strip of shops, as he does every time he passes it. The art council commissioned Bart Tucker to interpret the essence of Fairmont and the result is perfect in Joe's opinion–a tender glimpse into the heart of an American town. The combination of the Dylan and the Tucker sends a chill down Joe's spine. He loves it when art and life collide.

Joe turns right toward First where Peggy and Tyler share a riverfront condo. Peggy is Joe's ex-wife. Though they divorced a decade ago; in the time since they have become the best of friends. Joe stops over for breakfast every Tuesday morning under the pretence of a weekly discussion about their twelve-year-old-son, Tyler. Really, they just like spending time together. Joe neglects to tell Tricia about these little meetings. He knows she wouldn't understand.

"Hey, Peg," he says as he opens the screen door without knocking.

"French toast all right?" she asks.

"Great," he replies, helping himself to a cup of coffee then taking a seat at the kitchen table. When they were living together, Peggy had worried incessantly about her weight and had dieted continuously. In their time apart her efforts have become less rigid. Joe likes her with a few extra pounds.

"Tyler tell you about the Pirates game Saturday?"

"Works for me," she says, approaching the table with two plates of battered bread.

Their conversation proceeds as usual: Tyler's teachers, Tyler's surprise comments, Tyler's Little League team, Tyler's first girlfriend, Peggy's sleazy hospital coworkers, Tricia's impromptu mood swings.

"Why do you stay with her, Joe, if she's really that tough to live with?"

"I guess I kind of feel responsible for her," he answers as he stands to leave. He was supposed to be at the bar ten minutes ago.

"You feel responsible for everyone, Joe," she observes in her warm, sandpaper voice. "You need to think about yourself a little more."

"Maybe," he concedes. "Why don't you and Ty stop by Friday night? Claire's playing."

"He wants me to take him to the batting cages," she replies. "Maybe after. If not, we'll see you here Saturday. Don't be late."

Donna sits on the curb in front of the bar with her hands submerged in her dishwater blonde hair. Joe smiles at her as he pulls up. They meet at the door, exchanging hellos, and he lets them in.

"How long have you been waiting here?" he asks in his perpetual morning voice. "I told you, you should always come a half hour late so you never get annoyed with me."

"I'm not annoyed, Joe. I like sitting on my ass all day."

"Hey, watch your mouth. This is a family establishment. By the way," he says, turning to her, "did something happen with you and Will the other night? I have a sixth sense about this stuff, and I get the feeling maybe something happened."

There is no judgment in his voice, only mild curiosity. His years behind the bar have taught him not to put anything past anybody and, most important, never to judge. Nobody's perfect.

"None of your business," she replies in mock indignation, obviously loving this line of questioning.

"C'mon," he pleads, playing along. "If you don't tell me, I'll fire you. I need to keep tabs on my employees."

"Nothing happened," she admits without much of a fight. "Will doesn't know that, though. He passed out cold."

"You mean to tell me that Will's walking around thinking he's the world's worst man, a complete and total asshole of a human being, purely for your amusement?"

He's actually a little annoyed with her now.

"I'll tell him eventually," she says.

"You're damn right you'll tell him," Joe replies.

"I just wanted to make him squirm a little," Donna asserts.

"I'll bet you did."

Donna proceeds to ready the bar for business as Joe disappears into the back office, as always.

🌰

Joe Camden Senior met Martha Reardon at a horse show in the summer of 1964. She sat perfectly straight as she guided her horse through the tricky obstacle course. He couldn't take his eyes off of her and cheered louder than anyone when the judges announced her blue ribbon. Afterward, he asked her to join him for dinner. She later admitted that "no" had never been an option, and that she had known, right away, as they stood in the harsh August sunlight, that she'd found her match.

This memory is okay, harmless enough. As Joe Senior bites into his chipped corned beef sandwich Tuesday afternoon, back on the porch, clean from the shower, he allows himself to follow it further down the path, to their wedding day, family and friends baptizing them in an ocean of thrown confetti. This one's okay, too–friends and family cheering them forward.

The following evening they walked on the beach in Wildwood, New Jersey, a Frankie Valli wannabe crooning in the distance. With his hands laced with hers and his heart racing he beheld eternity in her eyes and tried to say so.

"I know, I know," she said, kissing him silent.

Martha was his better half–plain and simple. Her smile could shield him from anything, even the memories he spends his days hiding from now. Mid-afternoon. Half way home.

He'll never make it.

Claire's there. Lindsay knows that. She wants more than anything to get a home run, like Laura just did, to impress Claire. For an instant, she fears that if she doesn't hit a home run, if she misses the ball and it falls to the ground as it has so many times before, Claire will like Laura more than her. That would be a disaster.

Focus, she thinks. That's the word Will told her was more important than all others when it came to hitting the ball off of the bright, orange cone. Focus. She's not completely sure what it means, but she associates it with squinting her eyes, which she does now as she grips the bat more tightly than she has ever gripped it before.

"Come on, Lin," she hears Will yell from the stands where all the parents sit. "Focus."

There's that word again. Okay. She's waited long enough. It's do-or-die time. After taking one last deep breath, she cocks the bat and swings it around with all her might.

"Casey at the Bat," she thinks. "That's who I am."

She can't believe it when she connects and, with a mighty thwack, sends the ball soaring through the air. She's never hit it through the air like that before. She fights her smile as she sprints around the bases, only vaguely aware of the left fielder's misfire to the infield, only vaguely aware of her audience's generous applause. She glances up at her mom and then at Will and Claire as she rounds third. Her gaze is drawn from them, smiling and cheering, to the man who sits beside them. He scares her. His eyes look like a wolf and a bright gold chain connects his belt to his front pocket. She feels him still watching as she crosses the plate and the coach gives her a high five. Her first home run.

"This is my friend Stanley," Will explains when Lindsay runs to them after the last out. "He's Joe's brother."

"Nice to meet you," she replies, forcing herself to employ the manners her mother is always harping about.

"Way to go, slugger," the mean man tells her in a slow, raspy voice that is every bit as scary as his eyes.

Claire leans down and squeezes Lindsay closer than even her mother usually does.

"Way to go, Lin," she whispers in the child's left ear.

"Who's up for Dairy Queen?" her mom asks.

Lindsay beams her response and drags her friends away from the scary man with the wolf eyes and the bright gold chain.

❧

It's uncanny the way Dominic's arthritis eases every year as summer approaches. It's as if his very bones know that the cold has departed for a time. Of course, the pain will return, a little sharper, a little deeper, with the autumn. But for now, he feels better than he's felt in months, not a day over fifty. He lies in bed praying as the predawn expands.

His prayers have evolved over time, away from the standard man-to-God dialogue he learned in Catholic school. Now he talks mostly to his wife, who left this earth seven years ago. Their years of sharing her gradual physical deterioration had prepared them well for her passing, and surprisingly little has changed in their relationship since she died. They still talk quietly over decaffeinated coffee every morning. They still share the same warm partnership and fun, gentle secrets.

Dominic puts in his dentures and pulls his trousers up over his dingy, pinstriped boxers. He steps out of the sturdy, two-story home he and his wife bought thirty-eight years ago when they were newlyweds, and he'd just started delivering mail. He can see sunlight in the distance though hardly any penetrates the thick roof of oak tree leaves and branches that shade Washington Avenue.

The Fairmont Tobacco and News is his Wednesday morning destination. He knows Hank Shaw would have hand-delivered a stack of this week's *Reporters* to the tiny, cluttered shop over an hour before. Dominic is amazed by Hank's tireless devotion to his weekly offering.

Dominic looks with disdain at the unshaven face and uncombed hair of the new kid at the register. He snatches a paper from the top of the pile and pays the ill-mannered runt, another one of the "artists" invading Fairmont. The town is going to hell in a hand basket.

Instead of turning left down Washington and returning home, Dominic continues straight and walks into the Fairmont Bakery, a bustling hub of early day activity. He is greeted warmly by the four middle-aged counter women, even as they wait on other customers. After getting his cup of decaf, he takes a seat at his booth directly in front of the side door. He pours some table sugar into his steamy beverage and turns his attention to the front page of the paper.

A MURDERER AMONG US?
The Moon Case Revisited
by Will Jameson

Why isn't he surprised? He knew something like this would happen. He knew they shouldn't have shared the story with Will. Why perpetuate the darkness and violence from which the town has never fully recovered? It was like poking an old wound with a rusty razor. Dominic feels a deep sense of foreboding as he pushes the paper aside.

"No good can come of this," he whispers to Maria.

3

Jessica Moon has been fucking John Parker on and off since she was seventeen. The fact that they have never had a meaningful conversation doesn't bother her in the least. They're not a couple. Hell, they're not even friends. Their bodies just happen to fit well together and, unlike most other men she's been with, he's able to make her come, consistently. She lies beside his big, snoring body now and stares out his bedroom window. Trees, sky, clouds: Fairmont in a nutshell.

Just before she met John Parker, in a bar, alone, on a Saturday night when she was four years under age, a boy in high school told her she was like a china doll, perfect and brittle and hollow inside. Though she acted unconcerned, his words affected her, which was more than she could say about anything else that happened in high school.

Jason Frey. That was the high school boy's name. He'd been the only person resembling a friend to her back then, his barely closeted homosexuality alleviating the tension that usually resulted from her looks. He even made her laugh sometimes, a rarity back then.

It's almost two in the afternoon. John, a card-carrying member of Fairmont's small, elite silver-spoon society rescued her from her dad's house the night before and they connected with a small group of his friends at a private room in the basement of the country club where they drank, played music and sniffed cocaine until dawn. It was like she'd never left Nashville.

John and Jessica returned to his place that morning and did what they always do, fucked. She knows her spent stud will stay sleeping until nightfall. He prides himself on seeing as little daylight as possible.

She slides off the bed and walks to the bathroom where she washes up and dresses. She doesn't regret having come here. She never regrets any of her actions. She simply regrets her life on the whole, and her station as the daughter of a world-class deadbeat and his infamous, disappearing wife.

Jessica climbs into the tiny sports car John has graciously loaned her, a small token of appreciation for the earthly pleasures with which she provides him, and drives off through the sparsely populated countryside above the town, beyond the mansions, through the maze of barren back roads. Her dad used to own a hunting cabin up this way, only farther. It had once been heaven to her but became hell at some point. The same could be said of Fairmont in general.

She gets back to Fulton, which she follows down to town. Before going home, she stops by Imperial's to pick up some dry cleaning. She leaves the car running in the four-space parking lot.

"What the hell are you looking at?" she barks at the old man she passes on her way into the store. "Moon," she says to the elderly woman behind the counter who, Jessica swears, is also staring.

"Moon," she repeats, handing over her wrinkled ticket stub.

As the woman shuffles to the ancient steel conveyor belt and punches in a three-digit number, Jessica's eyes are drawn to the stack of newspapers in the rack by the counter. The *Riverside Reporter*. The words are not yet in focus. She lifts off the top copy and settles in on the headline. Her heart pounds so hard she can hardly breathe, and the color drains from her face. Without her clothes, without a word, she storms out and heads for her father's favorite watering hole.

There are no words for her anger. Her expression says it all. The four men and one woman in the bar look terrified of her, as if she's a volcano whose eruption might badly disfigure them.

"Do any of you know Will Jameson?" she asks.

No one answers, but the three men at the bar all seem to be looking at the bartender.

"Are you Will Jameson?" she asks, locking him in her sights. "Who the hell do you think you are?" she shouts with all of her considerable venom and lifts, and then hurls, the object nearest to her—a heavy, glass ashtray, which grazes its intended target. As the asshole falls to the ground, Jessica screams, "Mind your own fucking business!" and heads for the door.

The ashtray nicks Will just above his right eye and caroms into the small collection of dirty glasses in the sink. He falls to the ground not so much from the impact as to escape further attack. Larry Paul struggles around the bar, atrophy in motion, and kneels beside him, reaching up for the rag that Donna has dampened with cold water.

"Will," he asks. "You all right?"

"What the hell was that about?" Will asks, struggling to an upright position. He'd only gotten to the bar twenty minutes before and is still unaware of his front-page status. "What did I ever do to her?"

He stands and leans against the counter, puzzled over this strange turn of events.

Before anyone can answer his question, Joe barrels through the front door and says, "Will, in my office."

Will follows, perplexed.

"What the fuck were you thinking?" he asks, the instant the door is closed.

"What are you talking about, Joe?"

"What the fuck were you thinking writing that article about Abraham Moon?"

Will's stomach drops as he forces his memory back two nights.

"What article about Abraham Moon?" he asks. Surely Joe couldn't have read it. He hadn't submitted the Moon article. He'd submitted an article about the President. He feels like he is starring in an episode of *The Twilight Zone.*

"The one on the front fucking page of the paper this morning," Joe answers, shoving a copy of the *Reporter* in front of his friend's face.

"Oh my God." Will's eyes widen. "What the hell did Hank do? He wasn't supposed to print this, Joe. I swear. He was supposed to print something else. I just wrote this for the hell of it. I never meant for anyone to see it. Hank must have looked through my personal folder. Jesus."

"This is going to piss off alot of people, Will," he warns, his anger fading. "Like Abraham Moon, for one."

"And his daughter," Will adds. "She just about took my head off with an ashtray. What should we do about Abraham?"

"Let's wait and see," Joe advises. "I doubt he'll even read it. I doubt he's a big Hank Shaw fan."

As it turns out, Joe's right. Or appears to be, at least. Two hours later, at 5:15 p.m., Abraham arrives as always and walks to his out-of-the-way table. If he did read the story, he seems utterly unaffected. Will is tempted to say something anyway, to apologize, but thinks better of it as he delivers the evening's first whiskey and soda. Maybe tomorrow. After his daughter's had a chance to share the bad news.

Will goes about his business, pouring drinks and making small talk, explaining himself to anyone who'll listen, but his thoughts are never far from the image of Jessica Moon, standing in the doorway, making her fiery presence known. Now that he knows what caused her ill temper, he admires her actions. She was standing up for her father. Maybe she wasn't such a terrible daughter after all. Just before seven, he picks up the phone and calls Claire who answers on the first ring.

"I'm not feeling too well," he tells her. "I think I have the flu or something. Maybe I should just stay at my place tonight."

Hearing Claire speak with concern and kindness, Will is overwhelmed with guilt but stays the course, forcing his attention past the blatant lie, past the thought of all she has just been through. What the hell is he doing?

She'll see him tomorrow, she assures him. She hopes he'll feel better then. He goes on to tell her about the mixed up articles and even about Jessica Moon and the flying ashtray.

"Be careful," she murmurs. "Get some rest."

He continues on his mission of mercy, looking through the phone book, finding the number for A. Moon.

"Jessica Moon," he begins, after she answers with an unfriendly hello. "This is Will Jameson. The guy you nearly knocked out a little while ago." Silence. "I wanted to apologize for what happened." Still nothing. "I never meant for that article to be printed. I swear I didn't." More dead air. "Do you think maybe we could get together and talk about it?"

"Why the hell would I want to get together with you?" she asks.

"I just want a chance to explain," he pleads. "It was all a big mix-up."

Click.

Without thinking, Will calls again. The moment he hears her pick up he blurts, "Please. Don't hang up. Just give me five minutes to explain face to face? I just want to apologize in person. I feel horrible about this."

She leaves him hanging, suspended in silence.

"In the park at midnight," she finally says. "I'll be the one smoking."

※

The guitar case is closed. Though Finbar has taken his black Martin guitar out to perform, he has not once done so in the privacy of his apartment. He has not strummed a single chord, sung a single note, for his own private comfort. The music that had been his blood has all but dried up, leaving just the shell of a musician.

Makenna is sleeping, still her primary hobby, and the apartment feels quieter than usual. Finbar unsnaps the gold clasps and lifts the brown lid. He pulls the beautiful instrument from its hiding place and rests it on his thigh as he sits.

E minor. That's the chord he chooses–sad and low. He strums it again and waits. Normally songs introduce themselves to him, shyly at first sometimes, but clearly, as if to say, "Hello, Fin, how are you today? Can you please write me now?"

He strums the chord a third time and waits again to see if anything comes, if anything beckons. He is met with the same black silence that has been his constant companion since Maggie's death. He can't imagine ever writing a song again.

The TV plays but the sound is down. Tricia sits at the flimsy living room card table and sips strong black coffee. The more she drinks, the wearier she becomes. Fatigue has worked its way into her bones.

Two memory strands alternate in her mind. The first is of her botched attempt to get closer to Will two days before. She frowns as she remembers his look of concerned disbelief. That's what it was. He simply wasn't buying her story. In her play to make him more of an ally, she effectively wiped away any chance of anything happening between them.

The next reel is equally depressing. It starts with the wide-eyed girl she had been, leaving the open-skied beauty of Northern California for what she thought would be the dark, urban mystery of a working-class town like Pittsburgh. She'd been accepted into the journalism department at a small college called Chatham, and felt intuitively like that was where she had to be–in spite of her parents' reservations.

"I just need to do my own thing," she insisted, oblivious to the tears in their eyes, the dread and pain in their facial expressions. "I feel like I need to be some place that's completely different from here."

Reluctantly, they acquiesced and put her on the plane headed east that August, four years ago. And at first, it felt like her instincts were right. She thrived as she explored Pittsburgh's nooks and crannies, loving all the ethnic neighborhoods, bridges and rivers in every direction.

It was smooth sailing until that fateful night at the start of her sophomore year. A folk singer she knew was playing at a dive bar in a little town about thirty miles away. Tricia jumped at the chance to attend with a small group of good friends. Those were the experiences she treasured, random adventures of discovery. With a smile on her face, she hopped in the back and went for the ride–like always. Wild, free Tricia.

Though she was only nineteen at the time, she bravely ordered a beer at the bar upon their arrival. Joe Camden looked her up and down with a smile she trusted instantly and said something about her looking closer to twelve than twenty-one, though he didn't say it in a mean way, clearly enjoying the sight of her. He let her fake ID slide and fed her beers all night, beguiling her with jokes and stories whenever he wasn't busy with other customers. She can't even remember now if she watched the set that night. She only knows that she told her friends she was staying over and would make it back to Chatham the next morning. Within a month, she dropped out of school and was living with Joe.

When she called home to tell her parents about the new developments, she heard surrender in her father's voice. She'd lost him. Only gradually did she realize her mistake, and by the time she did, Joe had built a wall between her and the world beyond Fairmont. Hell–the world beyond these dingy apartment walls.

How did he do it? She asks herself that at least a dozen times a day. How did he manage to cut her off from her friends, her family, and, most tragically, her real self? She supposes it was the one-two punch of winning her trust then stripping her self-confidence. Was she putting on weight? Why was she wearing her hair differently? Was that supposed to be funny? It got to where she didn't trust herself to talk with people, to engage in life.

Will was the exception. When he had come along two years ago, his friendship had been like water in the desert, a ray of light in a world gone dark. She instinctively trusted him and somehow overcame the wall of inhibitions and insecurities Joe had been building around her. Will gave her something to look forward to, reprieves from the deepening isolation. And now he too was lost.

Will often comes to Riverview Park, sometimes to run, sometimes just to sit and read. This is his first visit in the dead of night. He navigates his way across the baseball diamond, past the equipment shed, down to the park that features a playground, tennis courts, basketball hoops, and a quarter-mile cinder track, all tucked neatly beside the rolling river. The glowing tip of Jessica's cigarette announces her presence on the wood bench nearest the seesaws and lion-head fountain. He sits down beside her. A steamer noisily passes.

"I don't know why I came here," she says coldly. "You had no right writing that shit."

"I know," Will replies. "I'm sorry."

"Sorry doesn't take it off the newsstand," she interrupts. "Sorry doesn't keep people from looking at me like I'm a fucking murderer's daughter."

"I don't know how it happened," he replies weakly. "I was talking with some of the guys at the bar..."

"Joe Camden, I bet. Biggest asshole in this fucked-up town."

"I stopped in the office and just started typing," Will continues, too distracted by his attempt to restore his own reputation to worry about defending Joe's. "But I knew I couldn't print it. I saved it in my private folder and sent a different article to Hank. I don't know what happened."

"Why did you write it in the first place?" she asks.

"It's what I do," he answers. "It's what I want to do. I want to be a writer."

"Well you can stop practicing with my life story," she says. "Do you have any idea how hard it was growing up here after everything that happened? I don't need reminders. The ghost of my father is good enough."

He can't stop looking at her. Her long legs stretch from the edge of the bench to the top of the fence in front of them. Her eyes shine like moonlight in a whiskey jar, along with her olive skin and her straight brown hair.

"I know I messed up," he concedes. "I'm sorry. If I'd known there was even a chance of Hank printing it, I wouldn't have done it."

Silence ensues. She drags on her cigarette. He swings his legs up to join hers on the fence. It's not an uncomfortable moment. Some part of him, the part that never loses objectivity, the part that is constantly writing his own life story, knows that her beauty is succoring him. It's the reason he's here–prepared to give her the benefit of every doubt, content to sit and smell her perfume and marvel at the length of her legs.

"Did your dad see it?" he asks.

"I don't know," she replies. "I barely talk to the man."

"I take it you're not real close?"

"You looking for your next big scoop, Clark Kent?" she asks, eyeing him suspiciously.

"I'm not a reporter. I'm just a writer."

"No, we're not close," she says. "He barely speaks. It's like living with a fucking monk."

"You've been away though, right?"

"Nashville," she replies. "I went to school there and just stayed after I dropped out."

"Why'd you come back?" Will asks, searching for a conversational flow. He lets his feet drop and squares his body toward hers.

"Why don't you just cut to the chase?" she asks, the viciousness returning to her voice. "Ask me what you really want to know. Is my father an evil murderer? Is my mother living in our basement or something?"

"That's not what I really want to know," Will insists, deciding if he doesn't exhibit some backbone he'll be in deep trouble. "What I really want to know is what the hell you're doing here in this town you obviously hate, with a father you can't seem to stand? What can I say? I'm curious by nature."

"I came back to Fairmont just to take a breath," she replies. "I lost my waitress gig and I didn't want another one. I wanted some time off. I figured free rent with my Dad would work. And it's the same thing as living alone pretty much. A friend of mine says she thinks she can get me a job in LA. I'll probably go there next. I'm sure as hell not staying here."

She rifles through her purse for her cigarette pack and lights up another. Her legs still stretch out before him. Her countenance still blazes.

"What are you doing here?" she asks, surprising him. He'd pegged her as incapable of asking questions about someone else. Of course, he'd also decided that he wasn't going to let that bother him.

"I'm from Michigan," he begins. "My mom still lives there. I skipped out of college too, sophomore year, and eventually met Joe Camden at a concert in DC. He offered me a job so I followed him back here. I thought working at a bar would inspire me or something."

"I guess it did," she interjects. "What about your father?" she asks. "Where's he?"

"He died when I was a baby. He was in the Air Force. After he got back from Vietnam my mom got pregnant with me. Just after I was born they sent him out to California to help test some new plane they were developing. He got killed in a freak accident."

"Sorry," she says, surprising him again.

"You get used to it," he says. "I'm sure you know. Like, I remember when I was seven, and there was a Cub Scout event that I was supposed to take my dad to. I was completely embarrassed that I had to take my grandfather. I hid it the best I could, but it crushed me every time something like that came up. But then I got stronger, I guess, less affected by it, or better able to brace for it and prepare. You know, close down the things you need to close down. I don't know."

He's not sure why he's telling her all this, but he can't seem to stop.

"Then there was some big deal that boys were supposed to bring their dads to at school, and I didn't even notice he wasn't there. You know? I'd finally made myself immune." As he says that last sentence, he remembers crying himself to sleep late that night when he realized what he hadn't felt, and sensing, in a way he could never quite force into words, that some stretch of emptiness had sealed itself off in him forever. Maybe it was that, that empty place, that lack of something inside of him that defined him more than anything else.

"Immunity has its perks," Jessica comments. "I'm kind of fond of it, myself."

"Do you remember your mom?" Will asks.

"Yeah, I remember her," she says. "I remember her screaming at the top of her lungs. Chain smoking. I remember weird things, like her standing at the ironing board, or sitting at our kitchen table in a bright red robe."

"Any good memories?"

"Not really. Not of her. Some of my dad, though, I think. He was actually an okay guy before she left. I mean he never talked much, but I remember him carrying me on his back all the time and teaching me how to fish and shoot a bow and arrow and stuff like that. The only good thing I can remember of my mom is this beat-up panda bear she gave me. I think she found it at her work. I loved that thing. I wouldn't go anywhere without it. I needed it beside me to fall asleep at night … 'til I was like twelve."

Will is hung up on the words "before she left." For some reason he thought she would leave her mother's disappearance, and her opinion about it, up in the air.

"What?" she asks. "Why do you look surprised? Did you think I thought he killed her?" He doesn't answer, struck silent by her bluntness. "He didn't kill her. He worshipped her. She just went away, that's all."

Still more silence. Will can't stop looking at her though. He has an impulse to comment on her beauty. He has an impulse to reach out and touch a strand of her hair. He's one giant impulse.

"So what do you like to do?" he asks. "Besides throw ashtrays at loser bartenders."

"Ride horses," she replies. "But I haven't done it in way too long."

Claire can't sleep. She hates to admit it, but she needs Will. She literally craves the warmth that she has come to expect from him over the past several months. She knows he's not feeling well and that his single bed has barely enough room even for him, but she doesn't care. She grabs her jacket off the doorway table and leaves her dark apartment.

She's feeling a little bit better, she thinks—ever since her talk with Fin. She's even looking forward to her gig this weekend. She always makes the mistake of imagining gigs ahead of time. Now, for instance, she sees Joe's bar in her mind's eye, crowded and silent as she works the microphone on her favorite ballad. You can hear a pin drop. It won't be like that, of course. People will talk. Glasses will clang at exactly the most inappropriate moment. But for now, as she walks through the warm late-spring night, the show is the best of her career.

On a more immediate level, she looks forward to seeing Will, just as soon as she makes it up to Sixth Street, turns left and walks the four short blocks to his place. Ever since they lost the baby, she's felt closer to him than ever before. She smiles imagining his body fitting perfectly behind her as they cram themselves into his tiny bed.

She opens the gate to the green fence that fronts his building and walks to the door. He gave her a key a long time ago. This is the first time she's ever used it. As she ascends the stairs, she passes Lindsay's place and hopes the little girl is sleeping all right.

Before Claire gets all the way up to the third floor, she knows something is wrong. There's no explaining it. Butterflies, not good ones, suddenly appear in her stomach, and dread replaces her eagerness. She can barely even acknowledge the shift before opening and entering Will's threadbare abode, his writer's refuge. She glances at the bed and is not surprised by what she sees. Nobody.

※

The kickball is a bomb. It looks like a normal kickball, red and round, but really it's a kick-activated bomb. Mommy is there and so are Claire and Will and the scary man, and none of them will believe her if she tells them that the kickball is a bomb. They'll think she's just a scaredy-cat. She has to play along. She has to kick the ball that Laura is rolling to her, even though it will explode, even though it will definitely kill them. Kill them all like in Afghanistan; like in Iraq. It's rolling. It's rolling. More slowly than any kickball has ever rolled. When it reaches her, she closes her eyes and scrunches her face and prepares for the explosion. As her foot meets the ball, she awakens. She can't remember what she was dreaming.

It's late. Exactly how late, she doesn't know. She won't allow herself to look at the clock. She never does. It's still dark, though. She can barely see the faces of the stuffed animals surrounding her.

Lindsay hears footsteps above but can't place them. They're definitely not Will's. His are heavy and slow. These steps are just the opposite. She decides the gentle, quiet scratches must belong to Claire. She hears the upstairs door opening and closing, and the soft steps grow louder as they descend. She's tempted to run outside and intercept her friend, see what's wrong, see what's happening, but her mother instructed her never to leave the apartment alone, especially after dark.

All is quiet again. Claire is gone.

Lindsay lies there quietly, trying to empty her head, like Will told her. She takes long, deep breaths and thinks about her toes tightening, relaxing; her feet, tightening, relaxing; her legs, tightening, relaxing. It's starting to work, she thinks, but her mind starts running again, and she pictures her daddy. If she lets herself, she knows she could easily start crying. She wonders where Denver is. That's where mommy says daddy went. Denver. She wonders why her daddy hasn't asked her to come see him there.

There's something in the way he steps around certain aspects of his life, leaves a chunk of his story untold, that alerts her to the fact that there's another woman. No doubt about it. Will Jameson has a girlfriend.

Jessica has played the role of the Other Woman many times before. In fact, it's her role of choice, relieving her of the threat of intimacy while distracting her from the ever-growing black hole at the core of her being. She falls into it now. Flirting, playing, using the power she knows she has over him, the beauty enough people have reacted to and commented on for her to trust as an objective reality.

And yet, that's not exactly what is happening. His description of adapting to the absence of his father resonated with her. And now she's revealing more than she ever has. She loves horses? She hates winter? She's not sure what she's doing with her life? She misses the way she and her dad used to be? What the hell is happening here? She is actually talking with the asshole who dredged up her painful past and she likes it. The sky turns from black to blue. Birdcalls replace the crickets' grating hums.

"Thanks for coming," he says as they reach her car, the only one in the gravel parking lot. "Thanks for talking."

"Just don't ever cross me again," she replies, opening the front door. "And don't think you're completely off the hook yet, either.

I'll have to think about an appropriate punishment." She lets this sentence, a kind of invitation, hover a moment in the cool morning air before ducking in behind the wheel. "See you 'round, Will Jameson."

Intoxicated. That's the only way to describe it. Will takes a moment to live inside this feeling. He knows it's all wrong. He knows Jessica is not the woman for him, or even the person he wants to believe she is. But he's intoxicated, and there's nothing he can do about it. Consequences be damned, he thinks, as he walks home.

He thinks about the stuff he'd said about his dad and about the way writing had been a way for him to reconstruct his own reality without so many empty spaces. He thinks of the way his mother, sensing the joy only children found with each new modest creation, had encouraged him, lavishing his stories and poems with high praises, encouraging him to enter contests and to believe in his own greatness. He needs to call his mom.

Thursday has officially begun. By the time Will gets back to his building the sun is up and people are leaving their homes for their jobs, their lives. As always, the instant he's inside, he walks to his desk and sits before his cherished typewriter, not thinking, not forcing anything. As always, he had armed the ancient battle-ax with a clean, white sheet of paper before his last departure. As always, the words pour out of him. What is different this time though is his subject matter: Jessica Moon–the saddest, prettiest girl he has ever met.

4

When Abraham was a boy, he and his parents lived in silence. Not hurtful silence, or even uncomfortable silence. Just silence. His mother would answer his infrequent questions but always succinctly and without fanfare. And though he was aware that most other parents and children spoke more freely, he didn't envy those people. He was content with his family, relaxed and secure. He didn't need to talk a million miles a minute.

His world was one of quiet, unshared wonders. The tiny tracks he'd follow through the snow on winter mornings; the surprising, warm breezes that signaled the beginning of spring and the menacing gray winds that ushered in summer storms; the veiny explosions of color that invaded the leaves each autumn. It all captivated him and his brain worked these mysteries like poetry or arithmetic.

The first day of deer season each year, the silence blossomed into exhilarating action. Abraham's dad and he awakened long before sunrise and drove up to their cabin in the woods where they dressed, side by side, in their orange pants and jackets. His senses were completely alive, though perfectly divided between nature and his father. One moment he would gaze across the crisp, snowy distance, tearful with the hope of spotting something, anything, and the next he would stare in awe at his father's smooth mechanics and effortless command of weapon and body.

The crunching of their uneven, unequal footsteps on the dead, icy grass accompanied by their steady breathing and his father's occasional instruction, gave the morning its only sounds. And though they weren't like other fathers and sons, in those perfect moments they shared a visceral knowledge of their bond and savored it openly, if silently. It was more than enough to satisfy young Abraham Moon.

He hasn't thought of his father, or of those hunting excursions, in years, but does now, as he sits on the edge of his well-made bed in what little light manages to permeate the blind slats and edges.

Jessica gets home just before seven. She doesn't try to be quiet. She doesn't care if she disturbs him or what he thinks of the hours she keeps. She doesn't care about anything.

Jessica.

There was a time when she was the most precious thing in the world to him; where one of her smiles would give him a week's worth of happiness.

"Look at me, daddy," she'd squeal and then jump off the dock into the lake behind the cabin. He'd smile and applaud, give her a score to beat on her next try. On weekends they would walk for hours through the woods discovering everything together, naming the world, one item at a time. They were a team, the two of them. She was the sunshine and he was the earth.

Abraham stands quiet as cancer and walks toward the room's only chair. With a smile on his face, he dresses for the day.

Lights. Coffee. Espresso tank. Register.

Some days Claire wishes for a customer. Not today. She sits behind the counter and thinks of Will. Her thoughts all lead to the same sad conclusions: he lied, he's cheating, she's wasting her time.

Other men have disappointed her. When she was at the University of Pittsburgh, she had a boyfriend for six months. He, too, had been the world to her at first but then his thinness of character emerged. She'd begun sensing the shallowness of his thoughts, the posturing of all his life stances so that by the time she'd caught him messing around with a girl who lived down the hall from her, she'd built up her protection. She'd escaped from that one before he did any permanent damage.

She isn't sure she'll be so lucky with Will. She'd really thought he was different–naturally deep and strong, real and reliable. He was the solid Oak she could lean on and be shaded by. He was the one she'd been waiting for. How could she have been so wrong?

Finbar and Makenna drop by at quarter past eleven. The baby sleeps quietly in her well-padded stroller.

"You like this?" Finbar asks, referring to the Damien Rice CD Claire has playing. The singer's plaintive wailing suits her mood perfectly. "He's so brilliant he bugs me," Finbar continues. "I feel like he might be writing all these sad, beautiful songs in a board room or a bank vault or something. Can anyone really be that over-wrought? I mean lighten up, dude, you have songs in pretty much every single movie made." Fin's attempt at cynical humor falls short. "You okay, Claire?" he asks.

"Not really, Fin."

"What's up?"

He rolls Makenna to the nearest circular, white table and takes a seat in the store's tiny coffee shop area. Claire sits down across from him. Damien sings sadly about a woman who teaches Yoga. Claire tells Finbar what happened the night before.

"I should have known it was too good to be true," she says. "I thought we were perfect together: no trivial stuff, no clinginess, two independent people in love with each other. What was I think-ing?"

"It's not your fault, Claire," Finbar says. "You were just thinking whatever came naturally. And I hate to be the voice of reason, here, but don't you think you should talk to Will before you hang him out to dry?"

She shrugs off this suggestion.

"I just know it's not good, Fin. I can feel it. Of course we're gonna talk about it. I just don't think he'll have a good excuse. I feel like such an idiot."

"You're not an idiot, Claire," he assures her. "You're just honest, and expect other people to be. That doesn't make you an idiot. It makes you a good person."

They go on to talk about other things: the Moon story, Finbar's upcoming tour, Claire's show at Joe's the next night.

"Think you could drop by for moral support?" she asks. "I'm dreading it, Fin. I hope Will and I talk before then."

"I'll try and make it," he replies, standing. "Depends on what my folks are up to."

Before he can take hold of the stroller's handle, Claire moves to him.

"Think I need a hug," she says and he pulls her toward him. It's a comfortable, natural moment.

"No need to explain," he replies. "I kind of needed one myself."

It's almost noon when Will awakens. His first thought is of Jessica Moon. He wants to feel remorse for what transpired last night but can't get past the giddiness. Twenty minutes later he steps out of his apartment to find Lindsay sitting on the top step.

"Hey, Lin. What's up?"

He sits down beside her, in no particular hurry to begin his day.

"Nothing," she replies. "I'm bored. Can we play?"

"I need to go do a few things, Lin," he answers amiably. "Maybe later, though. I need some sweet revenge from the other day."

He elbows her gently, making her smile.

"I heard Claire in your apartment last night," she announces. "How come she was there when you weren't?"

"Claire?" Will asks. "Are you sure it wasn't Joe, Lin?"

"Your boss who gives me toys all the time?"

"Yeah, the nice guy with the toys."

Joe, a firm believer in going the extra mile for a good joke, had been known to stop by Will's place and type comical, often times pornographic sentences onto Will's blank typewriter pages.

"No, it was definitely Claire. I know Claire's footsteps."

Will is stunned. When was Claire there? He tries remaining focused on Lindsay.

"And why weren't you asleep?"

"Bad dream," she says.

"Another bad dream?" Will asks. "I promise you that bad things aren't what usually happen, Lin. Does that make sense? The stuff you see on TV seems to be happening everywhere, all the time, but really it's pretty isolated and rare. You need to think happy thoughts about the things you like to think about, Lin. Like ice cream and T-ball home-runs and beating me at basketball … and going to movies with Claire."

Claire. Claire. Why would she have stopped by last night of all nights? She never stopped by. Ever. Now she knows he wasn't there. She knows that he lied to her. She probably thinks that he is having an affair. Is he having an affair?

"I gotta go, Lin," he says, hurriedly extending his fist. "See you later."

He drives down Pennsylvania and turns left on Allegheny. He is agitated, an unfamiliar state for him, and still stunned by the fact that Claire would pick last night to make use of her key for the first time.

He'll go there now, he thinks. He'll tell her everything, admitting to his lie, asking her forgiveness. He rehearses the words in his head. "I need to tell you something, Claire. I kind of lied to you last night …" She doesn't know that Lindsay tipped him off. She'll think he's coming clean, being righteous in a hesitant, male sort of way.

There's no space available on his side of the cobblestone street. As he passes the shop he looks in and sees Claire and Finbar embracing. They stand by a table, a stroller at their side. Angered by the unexpected sight, he decides they'll talk later.

The Wilson Branch of Carnegie Library is not far from the hospital where Claire and he had gone just six days before. Six days. It feels like a month. Will hadn't planned on taking 28 North up to Wilson, yet here he is. He can't explain his compulsion to research the mystery that has made him the talk of the town. Part of him wants to forget he ever heard about Beverly Moon, but another part—the part that's putting quarters in the meter and walking up the stone steps—is compelled to find more. Maybe it's Jessica. Maybe it's that first novel.

Moments later he sits staring at a computer screen scanning the archives of the *Wilson Herald* for January 1989. The first thing he discovers is a short article that appeared on Tuesday, January 30 of that year. It reads:

'Red Flags' Increase Concern for Fairmont Woman

Authorities suspect foul play in the disappearance of a 29-year-old Fairmont woman who was reported missing Monday by her husband, the Wilson County Sheriff's Department reported.

Officers were searching Monday night for Beverly Moon said Maj. Bruce McKinney of the sheriff's department.

"There are several red flags that are causing us to suspect foul play," Major McKinney said.

The woman's husband, Abraham Moon, told officers that the last time he saw his wife was midnight Friday when she walked out of the house following an argument, Major McKinney said.

In the next day's follow-up, a head shot of Beverly Moon, taken in high school most likely, appears beside the text, which states:

Investigators to Use Dogs as Search Resumes for Missing Woman.

Wilson County authorities planned to use trained dogs today as they resumed their search for Beverly Moon, a 29-year-old mother of one who disappeared Friday after what her husband described as a quarrel.

About two dozen officers from the Fairmont Police Department and Wilson County Sheriff's Department combed the woods behind the Moon house but found no clues, said Maj. Bruce McKinney of the Wilson County Sheriff's Department. Authorities plan to return today to question people who may have been in the area when Mrs. Moon disappeared.

The sheriff's department has repeatedly said the husband, Abraham Moon, is not a suspect.

Mr. Moon, 29, is employed by the Edgewater Iron Works. He was not at his home Tuesday and could not be reached for comment.

Mr. Moon hired attorney Barney Lee of Wilson Tuesday.

Also on Tuesday, deputies searched the Moons' car and the residence a second time and took items with them, Major McKinney said. Lee said investigators took a handgun licensed to Mr. Moon along with a hunting rifle.

Mr. Moon reported his wife of ten years missing Monday.

Mr. Lee stated Mr. Moon believes his wife will return. He said his wife has left home before, and Mr. Moon only reported her missing this time because she did not go to work on Monday.

Major McKinney said authorities are considering Mrs. Moon's disappearance suspicious because she left her home without her keys or license, which were found in her nightstand. Friends and co-workers have not heard from her, Major McKinney said.

The couple's six-year old daughter was staying with her grandmother for the weekend and was not home during the argument that Mr. Moon said prompted his wife's leaving.

Mr. Moon offered to meet with investigators Tuesday morning at the family's house on Twelfth Street in Fairmont, according to Fairmont Police Chief Trevor Sykes. But Mr. Moon sent his attorney instead. Otherwise, Mr. Moon has cooperated, Chief Sykes said.

The Moons were married in 1979. Mrs. Moon works as a seamstress at Imperial Dry Cleaners in Fairmont. Mr. Moon has worked for Edgewater Iron Works since 1977.

The third article featured a photograph of police searching woods and focused more on Abraham than Beverly.

Fairmont Man Denies Link to Wife's Disappearance

The husband of a missing Fairmont woman said Wednesday that he didn't have anything to do with his wife's disappearance and thinks she'll reappear soon.

"There is absolutely no involvement on my part regarding the disappearance of my wife," Abraham Moon said Wednesday, in a prepared statement that he read in his lawyer's office. "I truly believe at any moment my wife will make her whereabouts known, as this is not the first time she has left."

His lawyer, Barney Lee, said Beverly Moon left in a huff three years ago and spent four days in a nearby motel without telling her husband where she was. Mr. Lee said he also thinks the 29-year-old mother of one will return any day.

The Fairmont Police Department and Wilson County Sheriff's Departments have joined forces, searching since Monday when Mr. Moon reported her missing. Authorities say foul play is suspected. The search expanded Wednesday when officers crossed into Sharpsburg and checked the shore of the Allegheny River under the Fulton Bridge.

Maj. Bruce McKinney of the sheriff's department said "a very credible source" reported seeing a vehicle similar to Mr. Moon's on the bridge Saturday. Searchers found nothing in the woods near the river or the woods behind the couple's house in Fairmont.

During ten years of marriage, Mr. Moon and his wife were never violent with each other except for one incident, Mr. Lee said. That incident occurred Friday night at their Fairmont house when Mrs. Moon told her husband she wanted to separate, according to Mr. Lee.

"He held her arm but she broke away." Mr. Lee said. "She scratched him on the face as she walked away."

Mr. Lee said Mrs. Moon walked out of the house, but her husband didn't pursue her because she often walked off her anger.

The sheriff's department declined comment when asked if Mr. Moon is a suspect.

Will continues scrolling for Moon articles, but he finds the same old details, hashed and rehashed. "No New Leads in the Moon Case." "Search is Continuing for Moon." "Fairmont Woman Still Missing."

As he returns to his car, Will pictures that night long ago. He sees the tree branches shaking in the bitter wind. He sees Beverly leaving the house without her license or her keys. He tries to imagine where she might have gone, but nothing comes. He wonders if Jessica has just grown used to a lie, accepting it eagerly since the alternative was so unpleasant. He winces, remembering again Claire's surprise visit to his vacant apartment.

Hank likes to mingle with his public on days after a hit. He considers it his civic duty. He walks into "Angelo's Italian Restaurant," beaming like a proud new father.

"Hank," yells the aging hostess Vivian from beneath the Coca-Cola chalkboard that bears the day's specials. "What were you thinking printing that trash?"

Hank smiles confidently, comfortable with his position at the center of the maelstrom, accustomed to controversy.

"The kid wrote it, and I felt it deserved to get out there."

He sounds hard-edged, hard-boiled, a cross between Sam Spade and Sam Elliot.

"Well it's all anyone's talking about," she reports.

She leads him to his booth in the busy eatery's elevated back room. A lime-green lamp lights the flowered tablecloth. Wood baskets and old metal pots and spoons adorn the wall to his right. The motif is mid-century kitchen cupboard.

"Hi ya, Hank," says Alfred Foley, a longtime fan of Hank's work, as he makes his way from the men's room to his table in the front. "You sure stirred it up this week."

"Just felt like it was worth revisiting," Hank says. "Didn't mean to stir up anything."

"Well you did," Alfred replies. "I just heard Ira Mendelson and Joe Camden's boy having it out in the bank. Feels like yesterday, don't it?"

Yes it does, Hank agrees, though he doesn't say so. He feels like the discussion has lasted long enough. He hates to let one person monopolize the conversation when so many are clamoring for his attention. Alfred gets the message and leaves him to his garden salad.

"He didn't do it, you know?" says the approaching waitress, Georgine Kassel. "I went to high school with them. He didn't do it. She left him for some fella from Wilson." Georgine breaks into laughter. "What am I thinking, Hank?" she asks. "You were in our class. You remember Abraham. He's no killer. A little bit of a weirdo, maybe. But no killer."

"I doubt we'll ever know, Georgine," Hank says.

"Yeah, you're right about that," she agrees. "We'll probably never know."

Hank returns to the office, and Irene hands him a stack of mail as he passes her station. Coffee after breakfast. Mail stack after lunch. It's how they've always done it. Back at the drawing board, he studies the top envelope before opening it. The return address says, "B.

McKinney." The name sounds familiar, but Hank can't quite place it. Inside, he finds a single-page letter that reads:

> Dear Mr. Shaw,
> I read the fine article your publication printed on June 17 and would highly recommend that you pay a visit to the Fairmont Police Station. You never know what you might find.

As Hank reads the puzzling words, he scans his memory bank for a B. McKinney. Finally, it comes to him. Bruce McKinney had been the officer in charge of the Moon case. He calls Information, which connects him with the Wilson County Sheriff's Department.

"Bruce McKinney, please," Hank says.

"Say again?" a pleasant deputy replies.

"Officer Bruce McKinney," Hank repeats.

Hank can hear the confused man push the phone away from his mouth and say to someone, "You know a Bruce McKinney?" When he rejoins Hank on the line he repeats the information he has just learned. "Bruce McKinney died ten years ago."

Hank rereads the mysterious correspondence then shoves it in the desk when he hears Irene greet Will in the outer office. Hank's instincts tell him that Will has come to give him hell for printing the wrong article. Hank is ready.

"Will Jameson," he bellows from the back office. "If it isn't my star reporter."

"Hey, Hank," Will replies. Hank can see the boy struggling to maintain his vengeful resolve. "I wanted to talk to you about that article."

"Yes, son," Hank booms. "Wonderful work. I can't remember when I've gotten so much feedback." This is a lie, of course. He can remember. It was twenty years ago when the Moon case first broke.

"About the article, Hank. That wasn't the one I wanted you to print. I'd appreciate it if you'd stay out of my private folders."

"Nonsense, Will," Hank insists, his face a pink sculpture of confused concern. "I printed the one you left on the desk, pal."

Will goes to the computer, opens his WORKS IN PROGRESS file and clicks on the article he'd meant to go public. Hank can see the thoughts buzzing in the boy's head. He almost feels guilty but not quite. In this business, sometimes the end really does justify the means.

"I meant for you to print this, Hank," Will states flatly, glancing toward the screen.

"You must have mixed them up, Will," Hank fibs. "Hope we didn't jam you up at the bar. I'll be happy to print this story in next week's issue."

"Whatever," Will replies, as close to anger as Hank has ever seen him. "I just wish you hadn't printed that Moon stuff, Hank. I didn't know what the hell I was talking about. It wasn't responsible."

"Of course it was, Will. I stand by every word of that article. And I should know. I was the one who first broke the story."

"Okay, okay, Hank," Will says, prudently surrendering to his superior's wisdom and experience. "Next time I'll just have to be more careful, I guess."

After Will leaves, Hank assures himself that it was right to keep the anonymous letter to himself. It's obvious that Will is not yet mature enough to handle so volatile a situation. It's Hank's baby. It's always been Hank's baby. Hank retrieves his precious communiqué from the top drawer and grabs a pad and paper. He hasn't felt so alive in years. Twenty years, to be exact.

He's too big for his britches. That's what Irene Turtleman thinks about Will Jameson. Oh, sure, he's easy on the eyes, and polite enough, but the boy is clearly an ingrate. How many writers get a mentor the caliber of Mr. Hank Shaw? That sassy pants has no idea.

She reaches into her purse and removes a tiny mirror. Dr. Phil says there's nothing wrong with looking your best, using your God-given attributes to their fullest. She reapplies the mascara the Avon girl assured her would complement her eyes and walks back to see if Mr. Shaw is ready for his end-of-the-day decaf.

＊

It's two in the afternoon. The room is black as midnight. What is happening to her? From the time she was a little girl, her mother and father would say, "She has a mind of her own, that one." Where has her fiery spirit gone? Where has she gone?

The phone rings. It's Samantha, from the bank. Tricia hasn't been to work since Monday morning.

"Tricia," her co-worker's friendly voice booms out across the stale, dank room. "You there?"

Tricia remains still and silent, twisted in a knot of dirty linen.

"Tricia," her colleague continues, "I don't know how much longer I can cover for you here. Greenwald's getting pissed. Tricia," she tries again, "pick up if you're there. Joe told us you're home."

Tricia can't move, let alone speak on the telephone.

"At least call me at home tonight," Samantha says, giving up for the third straight afternoon. "I'm worried about you. See you tomorrow."

Tricia can't imagine herself going to work tomorrow. She can't even imagine getting out of bed. Tricia can't imagine ever being that happy little girl again.

＊

One long-ago morning in the autumn, the dog that lived at 117 Twelfth Street nearly ripped off Dominic's leg. It was Dominic's first day on a new route, and no one had warned him about the vicious black Doberman. He narrowly escaped the dog's wrath and stopped to catch his breath beneath the next-door neighbor's green tarp awning. It was the Moon house.

It's funny how the details stay with him. Strange details. Things he would never notice now. The orange rust–shaped like the state of Florida–that showed on the railing where the paint had chipped. The curiously pristine "Welcome" mat upon which he stood. The sense that his left shoestring was loosening though it was still tied and looked secure. He remembers these things still.

He had seen Beverly in the same way he had seen everyone in Fairmont. Driving, walking, passing him by. In the outermost periphery of his town vision, it seemed like she had gone directly from childhood to being with Abraham, the quiet kid who loved to hunt. They had never had a conversation, though, Dominic and Beverly. They might not even have known each other's names.

"You all right?" she asked when she opened the door that sunny day in October, startling him. "That dog's got a screw loose, I think." She wore a red robe and smoked a cigarette. She was pretty—beautiful, even. But not like a movie star. More like a painting, he decided. Her lips were painted bright red. "You want to come in for a second? Have a glass of water?"

"Yes, thank you," he replied, following her, laying his mailbag on the chair beside the panda doll.

He was happily married. His wife, Maria, was his joy, his soul, and he loved her with all his heart. They had recently discovered that they couldn't have children. They would never have children. Maybe that was why he noticed the smell of this strange woman's perfume and the sway of her hips as she sashayed ahead of him.

They stood in the kitchen. She let the faucet water fill the tall glass then handed it to him, saying, "Dominic, right?"

Why was he flattered that she knew his name? He was too old for her. Ten years at least, maybe even closer to twenty. He was happily married, for God's sake. He couldn't imagine what he was doing there, just after ten in the morning according to the wall clock that ticked loudly behind her. He had to get back to his new route. It was his first day. He couldn't afford to fall behind.

"Yes," he replied.

"Beverly," she said, and waited for him to finish his water, which he gulped down. Their hands touched when he handed her the empty glass, incidental contact that sent a shiver from his fingers to his crotch.

She stood close to him, reached for her robe's red drawstring and pulled on it, revealing the front of the naked body underneath, not thin, but not heavy. A faint brown birthmark the size of a nickel was on display above her left nipple. A plain yet beautiful woman.

He remembers all this now as he leaves for the bar Thursday afternoon. As he always does when distracted by this perilous train of thought, he prays that Maria cannot read his mind, though he knows that she can.

Joe Senior won the bar in a poker game in the spring of 1971. August Monroe had been sure his friend was bluffing and followed eagerly as Joe continued to raise the stakes. Before they knew it, the bar was in the pot, and the friends weren't feeling quite so friendly any more. As it turned out, the new father, known more for his inability to win at poker than for the opposite, wasn't bluffing. His royal flush practically burned a hole in each of his fingers until he finally set it down. A winner.

He renamed the old, wooden watering hole "Joe's Place" in honor of his new baby, Joe Junior. His friends had, of course, insisted that was a pile of shit and that he named the bar in honor of himself. Only he knew the truth.

Only he knew the truth.

He stumbles into that sentence, a surprise insight, but backpedals frantically. He forces his thoughts back to the early 70s, still safe, still clear, as the bar became home base for the "hobby" that would lead to his fortune. He became Fairmont's lone bookie, the only game in town, the only game in all of the small surrounding towns, too. If you wanted to bet, you called Joe Camden. It was that simple.

By the time the authorities became aware of his illegal enterprise, he had already translated his ill-gotten booty into a modest fortune courtesy of the U.S. Stock Market. The richer he got, the simpler his existence. The bar. Their sons. His friends. Hunting. Martha. It was a simple life, a good life. The King of Fairmont.

The Pirates are sticking it to the Marlins – final game of the four-game series. Maybe they're finally rounding the bend. He's tempted to call the bar to see if the guys are watching but decides against it.

Though he did speak with Joe Junior last night – their Wednesday conversation. His eldest son told him how Will Jameson accidentally made Beverly Moon's disappearance the talk of the town again twenty years after the fact. Twenty years. It felt like yesterday.

As the sun begins to lose its battle for the sky, Joe Senior feels himself slipping. It's Beverly who leads him there, Beverly and Abraham – all part of the same dark web, if only in his head. He cracks the bottle of whiskey he swore he wouldn't drink until the weekend and surrenders to his memory.

*

Joe drives aimlessly. This is how it always begins. He finds himself needing to just disappear from his life. He cruises the streets of Wilson, happily taking in the pleasant summer-day scenes: mothers with children, mail carriers in shorts and short-sleeves, teenagers skateboarding. Passing the library, he sees Will's beast of a car parked outside.

"Bastard," he says, knowing that the young writer is still tracking down the Moon story, even after Joe had forbidden him to do so. More proof of Will's cockiness, as if Joe needed any.

Frill's Pub sits at the edge of town, on the stretch of road that boasts no shops or restaurants, just gas stations and bars. Joe is known here, but not by everyone. Normally he'd go further, up to Riverdale or beyond, but today is different. He can't say why.

He left Donna in charge of the place – a first – knowing that Will would be in at four and that most of his regulars didn't show up until later anyway. He had to get away for a while. Things were starting to get to him. Tricia, mainly.

"What'll you have?" asks the tall brunette behind the bar.

Joe carefully considers his answer. He loves these moments between strangers in which there is only potential and mystery, nothing else. She doesn't know him from Adam and, based on the absence of any left-hand finger jewelry, he'd say she's at least somewhat available.

"That depends on what you're offering," he replies in his friendliest, most innocent, non-threatening voice.

This is the telltale sign. Will she flinch or will she follow? You never know what might happen next.

"A little whiskey might take the edge off," she replies.

Following, definitely following. And dangerous, too. She turns, walks to the shelf, and pulls down a bottle of Southern Comfort. She sees him in the mirror he knows, admiring her but not ogling—it's a fine line—and he's certain she approves. He can feel it. Jesus, he is lucky with the ladies, in spite of his average looks, or maybe because of them. The harsh liquor burns a path down his throat and into his bloodstream.

"So where is everybody?" he asks.

"Lunch crowd's gone, work crowd's on the way. Why?" she asks. "Don't you like being alone with me?"

Open flirtation. A good sign.

"No, of course I like being alone with you," he protests. "In fact, I think you should lock up and we should get out of here." His mind flashes on the image of the two of them driving a little-known country road not far from there. It's important to visualize.

"Somehow I don't think my boss would agree."

"Tell him some guy went into epileptic convulsions, and you had to take him to the hospital. You had a clear choice: keep the bar open, or save the guy's life. My name's Joe, by the way," he adds, enjoying her smile.

Before she can reply, the front door opens, and a man Joe recognizes from his high school days enters.

"Hey, Sally," the burly intruder bellows, solving the mystery of her name, then adds, "well, if it isn't Joe Camden."

"In the flesh," Joe responds, the mayor again. So much for strangers passing in the late afternoon he thinks. "I'll have another, please, Sally."

Oh well. She's a little too old for him anyway.

❦

There is a certain bench in Riverview Park that Claire has claimed for her own. It's the second in the spaced-out group of four that face the river. She used to go there weekday mornings after eight o'clock mass during her "holy period" but now comes only when time allows her the indulgence of reflection. She swears the bench–the actual wood, screws and metal–is of divine origin. The mere act of sitting on it inspires prayer and meditation.

Thursday evening this is her destination. This is the spot she has chosen for her final farewell. She walks slowly along the railroad tracks and finds her way down, over and down until she reaches it, an hour after dusk. She is thankful for the darkness and for the absence of other late-day park users. She is thankful for little else tonight.

She has brought a bag with her, a brown, paper, grocery bag she sets on her bench now. Solemnly she takes out it's contents, a one-foot-tall, thin-branched seedling and a shiny hand shovel she picked up that morning at Lane's Hardware, and walks ten steps back into the grassy knoll she just crossed. She kneels on the ground and commences to dig a small hole. She tears the plastic from the base of the plant and shoves the soiled root into its new home, where she hopes it will grow and grow into a large tree that offers shelter and drinks up rain and sunshine.

This is her baby's funeral. This is the private memorial service for her broken promise of a future child. She wishes Will was with her, then curses her own weakness. She weeps beside the scrawny sapling. After she completes her task, she sits on her bench awaiting consolation.

❦

Jessica can't decide between the tight-fitting short-sleeve chenille and the much more down-to-earth blue and white flannel. In spite of the fact that she pegs Will for a natural, outdoorsy type, she opts for the former. Sexy is always best. Her faded Levi's will provide an effective counterpoint.

What a switch this is. Never before has she worried about what she looked like or plotted to win a man's attention. It's always been the men throwing themselves at her, boring her to tears, buzzing around her like moronic bumblebees.

She picks up the phone but thinks better of it. She has to play this right, use her looks, her presence, to full advantage. If she can only get him into bed, she'll have him. She'll fuck away the memory of every woman he's ever known, including the invisible girlfriend. Then she can leave town with a sense of accomplishment at least.

🌿

Hank Shaw is working late. He's decided to spend the day going over his old articles, reacquainting himself with the facts of the case. He'll visit the police station in the morning. A host of ancient articles is spread out before him. The Moon mystery. How many small-time, small-town journalists get to sink their teeth into a story like this one? It's a career maker and will certainly be his legacy to Fairmont, his insights on and perceptions of Beverly Moon's disappearance.

His thoughts have turned, though, not to that bitter winter twenty years ago but to a more innocent time further down the road of his memory. In his mind's eye, he sits with his mother on New Year's Day, sophomore year, high school. His father has recently died. No relatives or friends have joined them for the holiday meal, same as the week before.

"What are your New Year's resolutions, Harold?" his mother asks him after thoroughly digesting a tiny piece of the small bird they prepared.

"No more sweets," he replies, patting his belly. "And I'm going to start exercising."

Last year it was study habits. The year before, his slackening religious faith. Now, as then, she nods her approval. She so loves this blessed, self-regulating child.

Later, on his bed with the door locked, he smiles with the innocent thrill of his deceit. Yes, he does plan to cut out the sweets, he wasn't lying about that, but his true resolution, the resolution of a shy and frustrated fifteen-year-old, is to do something he has never done before: kiss a girl. Yes, it is time he became more acquainted with the fairer sex. And not just a normal kiss like he gives to his mother before she goes to sleep—a passionate, open-mouthed kiss that will change the course of his life. He gives himself until the end of the school year—roughly five months—to do it, to choose his prey and devour it. And you better watch out, because when Hank Shaw sets a goal for himself, he damn well accomplishes it.

He carries this resolution with him into the second semester, through the winter freeze and the spring thaw. He's certain people look at him differently, intuiting his resolve. He hints at his bold endeavor to his best friend, Andy Green.

"There are big changes on the horizon, Andy," he declares as they walk home from school together. "Big changes."

"Big changes, my butt," Andy replies, a doubting Thomas, not wanting to face the implications of his smarter, more handsome, better groomed best friend's mysterious pronouncement. "Big changes like what?"

"Big changes. That's all," Hank replies.

It's a Tuesday in March when it hits him. Fourth period study hall. He's been racking his brain all year for the right person to set his sights on when the answer was right there all along. Beverly Insagna. Two seats in front of him. Sure, her hair's a little greasy and her wardrobe leaves something to be desired, but underneath it all, she is a very pretty girl. Nicely developed, too.

Beverly Insagna. He's noticed her before, of course. They've been classmates for almost three years. She is like him in many ways. A loner with few friends. An outcast whose attributes are easily overlooked by the average Joe. A person who doesn't find it necessary to talk all the time or be the center of attention. Of course, she is the perfect choice. And he's never seen her with another boy.

Day after day he plans. And as he plans Beverly transforms from the girl he's chosen to receive his first French kiss into the woman of his dreams. So vividly does he fantasize scenarios–long, detailed scenarios beginning with the kiss then covering years and separations and trials and tribulations–that he begins to take them for granted and accept them as real. She is his girlfriend, fiancée, wife, child-bearer and cemetery neighbor. She is his everything, and this before they have even shared a conversation.

But that will change soon enough. The notes he's been leaving seem to be doing the trick. Beverly has taken to wearing lipstick and nicer clothes, and her hair seems to be styled a little differently. He is astonished and thrilled that his words, his actions, have brought about this change in her. He shoves modest little notes into her locker each Friday afternoon so she'll have all weekend to savor them and wonder about the mystery man leaving her anonymous love poems.

Roses are red,
Violets are blue,
I spend my nights dreaming
Of beautiful you.

Then:

Lately I've been lonesome
Swear I'm at my wit's end
Need a one and only
Would you be my girlfriend?

He can't believe he's doing this. He is impressed with his own bravery. He enjoys writing his articles for the high school newspaper, but they don't provide a fraction of the pleasure that the poems do. Of course, he doesn't tell anyone. Not Andy. Not his mother. He fears he might diminish the thrill by sharing his adventures with another living soul. Instead, he grins until his face hurts and walks on air from class to class. He has never been so happy.

Finally, the decisive moment arrives, the Friday of the Spring Dance. He's known all along that he couldn't lose sight of his goal. No matter how fun the chase was, he had to reach the finish line. On this beautiful, cloudless Fairmont afternoon he leaves his final note:

Beverly, oh Beverly
Your beauty I have seen
Come to me at ten o'clock
Outside of 219

He can barely contain his excitement at dinner. His mother asks him what the devil has gotten into him and he grins, not answering, forcing food into his mouth. He wants to say, "I have found my true love, mother, the woman with whom I will spend my days and nights. Nothing will be the same after tonight." Instead he chews and he chews and he swallows and he doesn't say a thing.

He dresses with more care than he has ever dressed. New blue jeans rolled up at the cuffs like all the kids are wearing. A short-sleeved dress shirt with a flashy design that seems to catch everyone's eye. His black hair parted in the middle for the first time, an outward symbol of his inward change.

He sneaks out the door just before sunset, not wanting to have to explain himself or his appearance to his mother who would never understand, not in a million years. He'll deal with her later, after his mission is accomplished. Nothing will bother him then.

He nervously walks the streets, not wanting to arrive at the dance too early, not wanting anyone to distract him from his romantic course. He has rehearsed his lines to death, of course. Nothing. Not a word, until after they kiss, and then he'll look her in the eyes and whisper, "Do you know how long I have wanted to do that?" She'll be speechless still, and he'll continue, "I love you, Beverly."

He looks at his watch. It's 9:45. Time to make his move. He walks the steps down from Allegheny and crosses the railroad tracks onto Freeport. He continues down Virginia and turns right into the high school parking lot. He walks bravely, resolutely, across the baseball diamond and soccer field until he reaches the school's glass back doors. He hears the commotion of his classmates in the gym below but doesn't go to join them. He has bigger fish to fry. He ascends the stairs past the first floor and rounds the bend onto the second.

The sight he sees then does provide a clarifying, defining moment. It will change his life, but not in the way he had hoped. Beverly is there, all right, but she is not alone. And, she's not with her girlfriends. She's with another boy. And she's not just talking with him. In fact, they're not talking at all. Beverly is locked in a kiss with Abraham Moon. Abraham Moon. He has never even seen her with Abraham Moon. He can't believe his own eyes. His heart squeezes up into his throat and tears burn through his sinuses.

"Wait a minute," he wants to scream at the top of his lungs. "That should be me kissing that beautiful girl. She's mine, not yours, Abraham Moon. That's Hank Shaw's girl you're kissing."

Hank turns, unable to watch the crushing spectacle any longer and runs back in the direction from whence he came. He makes it down three stairs before he begins to tumble. When Principal Wheeler finds him ten minutes later, his right collarbone is broken and his pride is wounded beyond repair.

A tear falls on the twenty-year-old newspapers Hank has set out on the drawing board. Wiping his eyes he gazes across the headlines he penned all those years ago, when the town turned to him for answers and clarity in a time of dark confusion. It's a small measure of compensation that, through her death, Beverly gave him the chance to be the kind of man she might have loved.

5

"Anybody see that game last night?" The question is posed by late-arrival Chuck Proffer, a member of the expansion regulars who join their comrades-in-booze Thursdays through Saturdays. Chuck is tall and thin with a lazy eye and an even lazier disposition. He works as the groundskeeper for Riverview Park. His crack staff of two makes sure the lawn remains tended and the litter is removed from the garbage cans in a timely fashion.

"Hey Donna, what are you doing later?" asks Larry Paul, who has talked all the baseball he cares to and would rather pretend he has a chance with the well-endowed waitress.

"Uh, I don't know, Larry," Donna answers in mock flirtation, "maybe we could get a room or something."

He knows she's kidding, and he doesn't mind. In fact, he likes it. It gives him some actual dialogue to chew on later, in the privacy of his efficiency.

"Hell, we don't need a room, darlin'. My bed'll do just fine."

"Where's Joe?" wonders Dominic, who's quieter than usual tonight.

"Took the night off," says Will.

"He was here earlier," Donna adds. "He might be back later."

It's a bad night for Joe to take off. Thursdays are always busier than the other weeknights, but tonight the place is jamming. Both pool tables are occupied and surrounded by challengers, and a large group of college students, home for the summer, has taken over the dining area and is monopolizing the attention of the part-time waitress, Ingrid Miller.

"Hey Woodward and Bernstein, who do I have to fuck to get a beer?" asks Tony Jones, employing the nickname he created an hour earlier for the world-famous reporting bartender. It's no funnier now than it was then.

Will is gradually realizing the impact his misplaced article has had on the town. It's as if all these people were just waiting for the floodgates to open again, so they could put into action all they have learned from years of Court TV and Primetime Live. They are all expert panelists.

Larry Paul imparts the little-known fact that both Beverly and Abraham were having affairs. Chuck Proffer states that he thinks he remembers hearing that Abraham bought fresh ammunition the day of the alleged incident. Tommy Malloy wonders if everyone knew that for years and years the Camdens and the Moons had hunting cabins next to each other and that Joe Camden, Sr. bought the Moon cabin from Abraham ten years ago. Ingrid Miller, in more of an expert witness capacity, declares that Abraham should have killed Beverly if she was cheating on him, and Donna reaffirms her opinion that Abraham is hot in an "old dude kind of way." Darren Smith recalls his sense that Hank Shaw had been "making shit up" in his coverage of the case saying, "The guy's a realtor. He should stick to realty."

"I worked with a guy at Ithaca College when I first started teaching," Bartholomew Tucker volunteers. "Everybody loved him. He was easily the most popular professor on campus. Well, it turned out the poor guy was an amateur taxidermist. He poisoned and killed his wife and had her mounted on the wall above his fireplace." This inspires groans from all in earshot. "So you just don't know what people are capable of," the painter concluded, the sparkle never leaving his eyes.

Perhaps the most credible participant in the evening's roundtable is Raylene Jenkins, who worked with Beverly for several years and may have been the last non-family member to see her alive. "She was having an affair," the heavy-set woman confirms. "She wasn't trying to hide it either. And you should have heard the way she talked about her daughter. You'd have thought little Jessica was a grown woman. It was like Beverly thought they were in a contest or something. It used to give me the willies.

"And I know this will sound crazy," she added, "but I swear I saw Beverly at a truck stop in Breezewood when we were driving back from Ocean City two summers ago. Or if it wasn't her, it was someone who looked just like her–in the passenger seat of one of those big eighteen-wheelers."

And so it goes. Townsfolk do what townsfolk do–they talk. Only Dominic remains silent on the subject.

✒

"Long night, huh, Willy boy?" Donna asks after the last drinker has left the premises.

"Yeah," Will agrees. "I wonder what Joe was thinking leaving us alone tonight."

"He seemed kind of stressed out. I think him and Tricia are having some problems."

As the two finish cleaning, Will withdraws into his private world of depressed distraction. It's hitting him now, the sad transformation his relationship with Claire has undergone in the past forty-eight hours, forty-eight hours in which they haven't even spoken. Everything has shifted. One minute you're in love, the next, you don't know what the hell is happening. What the hell is happening? He needs to talk with Claire.

"You can take off if you want to, Donna. I'll finish up here."

"You sure you don't need a ride or anything?" she asks with a sly smile. Their time of awkwardness has passed, and they've returned to their previous roles.

"Yeah, I'm sure," he replies, smiling as well. A ride is the last thing he needs.

"A bunch of us are going over to Bart's," Donna says. "He's unveiling a new creation. He says it's his war protest painting."

Though Will loves the impromptu late-night gatherings at the painter's riverfront condominium, he nods his head in the negative saying, "Not tonight, Donna."

"Okay," she says. "I'll see you tomorrow."

Before departing, Donna turns and says, "By the way, nothing happened that night at my apartment."

Will doesn't say anything. This little tidbit of information would have meant the world to him just days before but is now low on his list of concerns. He hears the door close behind her as he empties the register and carries the black bag of bills to the office safe. When he returns to the main room he is surprised to find Jessica leaning against the bar. She is even prettier than he remembered.

"Hey," she says.

"Hey."

"Want some company?" she asks.

"Sure," he replies, unable to say anything else.

⚜

Dominic watches from the bus shelter as Jessica leads Will to John Parker's tiny sports car. The sight does little to ease the melancholy that has owned him since the article first ran. Over time he had trained himself not to think about her, not to wonder. He had let the whole sordid interlude disappear from his inner sight. No longer. He feels himself surrendering again...

Mondays and Thursdays. Those were the days Beverly worked twelve to nine, not eight to five. Those were the days they would meet – after some agonizing, of course, and some hard-lost arguments with himself. He'd race through the early portion of his route to make sure they'd have time together. He'd deliver their mail as he would any other family's, then turn left into the Nature Preserve and cut through the backyard under cover of the dense trees at the rear of their house. He became less and less mindful of his carrier duties, always sacrificing accuracy for speed. Monday after Monday, Thursday after Thursday, he ran to Beverly, seeking the water she continued to offer.

She was nothing like Maria. She was nothing like Dominic, even. She inspired a desire in him, an abandon, the likes of which he had never known. She used words he'd thought were reserved for barrooms and urged him to do things he hadn't known were options. With both hands, she would guide his head down the length of her body, where he would nuzzle and burrow and blindly follow his animal instincts. She might unexpectedly push him onto his back and mount him, then plead with him to get behind her, to move slower, faster. And he complied gladly, a quick study eager to share his newfound knowledge. They made love on countertops and toilet seats, in shower stalls and closets, grinding and thrusting, devoid of self-consciousness, moaning some new language.

Afterwards, her passion would return to hiding behind a cloud of cigarette smoke. It was in these quiet times that he pieced together her life story.

"What was your childhood like?" he asked one morning two months into their affair.

"I never had one," she said. "When I was four years old, my parents stopped talking. My dad moved down into the basement. He got workmen's comp or something. He'd get checks in the mail every month that he'd use to buy beer and whiskey. I hardly ever saw him … or even heard him. My mom and I had to take care of ourselves. When I was in the second grade, I started working with her in the tailor shop, cleaning and sewing and doing whatever needed done. Mr. Anderson paid me a dollar a week."

Her voice was soft, lilting, soothing to his ear. He'd stare like a child at her lips as she spoke, absently stroking the curve of her waist as if to smooth the already smooth skin there.

"I didn't have any friends. I just went about my business. School. Work. Nobody bothered me."

"How did you meet Abraham?" he asked. He'd been wondering how two shy introverts ever managed to make each other's acquaintance. Though Dominic was somewhat quiet himself, his courtship with Maria had been fairly traditional: flowers, letters, moonlight serenades.

"We went to high school together," Beverly continued. "Junior year, he wrote me a few poems and snuck them into my locker. Actually, he confessed to me later that he'd paid Hank Shaw to write them for him ... but still, no one had ever thought of me that way."

Her ceiling gaze betrayed some faint hint of sentiment that filled Dominic with surprise jealousy.

"Now, he hardly ever talks," she said, after they'd both put on their underwear. "He doesn't mean anything by it. He just doesn't know how. We go days without saying ten words. Jessica doesn't seem to mind. They have their own little silent language. She's always giggling at him like he's the funniest man in the world. They're cut from the same cloth, those two."

Dominic had tried not to think about Jessica, a child who lived under that same roof, who needed two parents to love and protect her. He chose to ignore what he heard in Beverly's voice when she said the girl's name. Not love. Not protection.

"Why do you stay with him?" Dominic asked.

"I'm waiting for something better to come along," she replied, the faint trace of a smile upon her lips.

And so Dominic came to learn the hardest of Beverly's lessons: it's possible to love two people at the same time. His love for Maria had not diminished. In fact, it had sweetened somewhat, its innocence heightened by the torrid nature of his new morning ritual. Yet, that love was overshadowed by the way he felt for Beverly. He craved her and became reckless in his need for her.

It was a time of hard lessons ...

Dominic watches as Jessica and Will drive away. He's amazed by how much she looks like her mother did back then. He stands and begins the short walk home, amazed at how history repeats itself.

❧

"Home sweet home," she remarks after parking directly behind her father's car, in front of their one-story house. Will is perplexed, and shows it. She laughs at his transparency. "Don't worry, Will, we won't go inside. I just wanted to show you something."

Jessica carries an Army-green knapsack and leads Will to the intersection, where she turns left. Moments later, they reach the mouth of the Black Hollow Hills Nature Preserve. According to the posted sign that greets all who enter, though, a plethora of exotic birds and wildlife coexist in this tiny patch of Western Pennsylvania forest.

"This used to be my whole world when I was a kid," Jessica remarks, leading him by flashlight down the covered path that only she can see into, the place where the moonbeams can no longer find them. "This and the cabin my dad's family used to own. Watch your step," she says after Will trips. "This way."

She turns, leading him between two overgrown trees among a thick, dense wall of them, into a small circular clearing.

"Man," he remarks. "Talk about hidden."

"This was my super-secret hideout," she explains. "I used to come here all the time when I was little. I'd sometimes mess with people visiting the preserve by climbing that tree and throwing little twigs at them, and they could never, ever find me. I was invisible in here."

She smiles as she remembers. A blanket appears from her bag, followed by two candles and a bottle of red wine. Her plan is to transform this hidden patch of earth into a motel bed or a spacious back seat. A sneak attack. She hopes that Will won't realize what is happening. She wants him to be surprised when suddenly faced with all the possibilities.

"So did your dad read the article?" he asks.

"You got me," she replies, handing him a tin camping cup of wine then pouring one for herself.

"You mean you really don't talk to him?"

"Not if I can help it."

"What did he do that was so terrible?" Will asks, definitely not adapting to the mood she had hoped to create.

"Nothing," she says, meaning just that. "You probably won't understand this. It started after my mom left. My grandma died a few years later, and there was nobody left. I didn't have any friends. The kids at school wouldn't talk to me. I needed someone, you know? And my father completely dropped the ball. He'd make me meals and stuff and buy me clothes at the beginning of each school year and all that shit, but really he disappeared when my mom did. By the time high school rolled around I hated him for giving me such a shitty childhood. You know? It was like one day I woke up and I wanted to kill the guy for being so miserable. I was a little kid. I needed a dad."

"Do you remember what he was like before your mom left?" Will asks.

"I know he was nice to me. I know I liked him way more than my mom. She's the one I remember yelling all the time." Jessica forces herself to stop speaking so openly. She needs to regain control of the situation. "Can we talk about something else?" she asks, forcing a smile and moving closer to him. "Have you started your masterpiece yet?"

"No, not yet," he replies. "I'm still doing the research."

That's better, she thinks as their legs touch, then their arms, intentional yet unintentional. Perfect.

"Does your mom ever get on you about finding a real career?"

"Not really," he says. "She worries a little, I guess. She just wants me to be happy."

It suddenly feels like a moment when Will might waver. Seducer's intuition. Jessica decides she better seize this opportunity while she has it. Their eyes meet and she maintains the contact even as she takes his cup and sets it on the ground beside her own. He has great eyes. Great hands, too. Upright, on her knees, she touches his cheek with the very tips of her fingers and moves her face toward his. Their first kiss is cold and tentative–metallic wine–but soon they gather steam. She welcomes his weight, which forces her gently back onto the blanket. She wants him to be on top of her. She can't remember wanting a man so badly. She lifts herself against his hands and is glad when he bypasses the gentlemanly outer grope and goes straight for skin, her belly, her breasts.

He smells it first. Smoke.

He rolls off her, and they stand and look in mild horror at the plaid blanket that has been set ablaze by an overturned candle. Will jumps from her side and stamps out the infant flames. They laugh themselves silent, knowing the moment has passed. Jessica feels the shift inside Will.

"Fuck," she thinks. "The invisible girlfriend."

Beverly Moon had been there the first time Abraham served as Joe Senior's lone guide, shortly after Abraham's father had passed. She didn't seem happy about it. She looked insolent, even, smoking cigarettes at the table as her daughter colored. That had been his only interaction with her, there in the modest cabin after he and Abe returned with the giant buck they bagged–the deer that solidified Joe Senior's belief that the young Moon was his good luck charm.

He said something along those lines to Beverly as Abraham tended to the dead animal–something about her being his good luck charm and how he hoped she came next time as well.

"All these years in the same small town," he said, "and we've never even spoken. That just doesn't seem right."

That's the part that makes him wince now. It was out of character for him–flirting with her like he did. Though he was supremely outgoing, seeming to thrive on interaction with others, his personality did not include a burning desire for female conquests. That was why it had taken him to the ripe old age of thirty to find a woman worth pursuing, a woman like Martha–ten years his junior, upon whom the sun rose and fell.

In Beverly's eyes, though, he saw something much different than what his wife's eyes held. He saw a power fueled by restlessness and ignorant of rules, a beauty built on sadness and reserved for no one. As she answered without answering and looked through him at the wall, out the window, he knew what her skin would taste like, how her head would loll, her hair would fall, as she mounted and strad-dled him. She was that kind of woman, the kind who could place impure thoughts in your head with a single sideways glance. He knew, just for a fleeting moment, that Beverly Moon could redefine pleasure. As he escaped from her that day, armed with fresh veni-son and false, phantom memories, he carried his new knowledge with him.

Joe is drunk. He drank all night—whiskey mostly. It's four in the morning when he stumbles into the apartment.

"Tricia," he barks, his voice thick and gravelly. "Get up, lazy bones!"

It's pitch black, but he hears her breathing. He swings at the wall switch and hits it on the second try.

"Get the fuck out of bed, Tricia," he yells again, more forcefully now.

She remains a motionless clump beneath the covers.

"All right, that's it," he warns, and rips the sheets off her. "This is for your own good," he assures her, lifting her limp body, carrying her to the bathroom and laying her in the tub. "We need to clean you up, little girl," he says as he points the showerhead at her face and turns the water on full blast. Even beneath the stinging barrage she refuses to open her eyes, the willful bitch.

"How pathetic," he thinks as he unbuttons and unzips his jeans.

Above dreaming; below consciousness. This is where Finbar meets Maggie each morning before dawn. Maggie comes to him like an-gels and says, "I love you. You're all right. You're all right."

He smiles at the sight of her and opens his arms to her undying beauty, her unwavering love.

"Where are you, Maggie?" he asks. "Where did you go to? How can I find you?'

"I'm with you all the time, Fin. Never stop knowing that."

It is always following this assurance that she floats backwards, a blinding light, away from him. She floats and she floats and then disappears and, as she does, the dam that holds his tears opens, and he cries for his awakening back into that world in which she no longer exists. Every morning, that is, except this one.

Today his eyes are dry. The face of Claire Jordan appears, uninvited. Finbar feels guilt, both for picturing Claire and for the absence of his tears. Why isn't he crying? Is his grief subsiding already? Never.

He gets out of bed and walks to the crib that stands four feet away. Makenna sleeps with her arms outstretched. Maggie's words come back to him: "You're all right. You're all right." Finbar knows this to be true. One sight of the peaceful child–heavy eyelids closed over innocent brown eyes; tiny, delicate lips and nostrils breathing sweet air steadily; small, blanket-covered chest rising and falling with the miraculous effort–and he is all right. Makenna will guide him. Smiling, babbling, crawling, standing. She is the face of God on earth. She is perfection itself. She moves him to prayer and unwanted comfort.

Minutes later as he dresses quietly, Claire's face reappears. Again, he feels guilty.

Early Friday morning, Lindsay stands on the grass beside her building and hits the wall, over and over, with the basketball. Chest passes, that's what Will calls them. She knows it's too early to be making so much noise, and that each thump will travel up the length of the building to where Will sleeps, and that Will got in late again, very late, but she wishes he would wake up and play with her. They never get to play together anymore. If the trend doesn't change soon she might be forced to play with Suzie Mitchell from down the street. The two had been friends when Lindsay first moved into the neighborhood, but that had faded as Suzie revealed her girlish tendencies–tea parties and Barbie dolls, while Lindsay was a committed tomboy.

She's tired again. She can't describe what happens in her head. For weeks, sometimes, she'll carry a feeling with her, a sense of things to come, a cloudy picture growing clearer.

It happened before her daddy left. Her parents never argued or raised their voices or anything. When she was with them they even smiled and played happily. But gradually, the image of him fleeing crystallized in her imagination and, sure enough, he did. One Friday afternoon two years ago, he knelt down in front of her as she sat eating lunch–peanut butter, no jelly–at the kitchen table. He had tickets in his hands and his face smelled fresh like in the mornings. She even knew what words he would say before they left his mouth. "Pumpkin, daddy's going away for a while, but he loves you very much." She could have spoken them for him. She could have told him he was going to start crying long before he did. Maybe then he would have stayed.

It happens with other things, too. Once, she awakened and told her mommy that she dreamed about a beanstalk with windows and elevators, and that she saw it burning and people screaming and rolling away on beds. Later that day, a big building in Africa was bombed. Her dream played over and over on CNN.

Another time, she had a stomachache for almost two weeks but knew it wasn't hers. Her mommy made her go to the doctor, but he didn't find anything wrong. She knew he wouldn't. Then daddy called and said there was something in his belly, and they had to cut it out of him. After that, the stomachache stopped.

For days now, she's had that feeling. Something's wrong. It's not only in her dreams that she sees it, but when she's awake, too. A fuzzy picture, like when the cable goes out, and the image of someone, someone she knows and loves is standing there. Mommy?

Claire? Will? She wishes it would get clearer, and yet that's what she fears the most. Something bad is going to happen. She'll wait until she sees it to tell somebody, to warn them. But for now, she throws the ball against the wall and hopes that her friend will wake up soon.

*

The Fairmont Police Station is on Fifth Street. It's an unimpressive one-story redbrick building. Hank enters it late Friday morning, a man on a mission. Dan Conway sits behind the reception counter reading the *Pittsburgh Post-Gazette*. The competition. Hank has caught Dan at the tail end of a Twinkie.

"Hey ya, Dan," he says with a broad smile.

"Hi, Hank," Dan replies cordially. "What can I do for you?"

"I was wondering if you could help me out with something," Hank says. "How far back do your records go?"

"Moon case?" Dan replies, reading Hank's mind.

"You read the article I guess."

"Didn't everyone?"

"What about those records?" Hank asks, knowing this is no time to rest on his laurels.

Without hesitating, the portly officer leads him through the nearest door and down a flight of stairs into the basement, where they find stacks of boxes, each one bearing the numbers of a particular year. Dan scans the piles and comes upon "1989," which he pulls down and sets on the floor in front of Hank.

"Knock yourself out," he says, passing Hank on his way to the stairs. "What are you hoping to find, if you don't mind me asking?"

"Nothing in particular."

The records kept by the Fairmont Police of 1989 are rudimentary at best; they read more like diary entries than official documents. But the Moon Case did garner more attention than the other suspicious activities that year. In addition to the "incident reports," there are photographs of the various rooms in the Moon house along with potential crime or disposal scenes. Also, there are transcripts of interviews with Abraham. Hank picks up the first sheet and begins reading.

INCIDENT REPORT FOR MONDAY, JUNE 29, 1989
This afternoon at approximately 1:00 PM a male Caucasian entered the station house and identified himself as Abraham Moon. He reported his wife Beverly Moon missing.

According to Mr. Moon his wife and him had an argument on Friday night and she left the house in a fit of anger. His face was scratched which he said happened when he tried to forcibly restrain her and she shook free of him, accidentally catching him with a fingernail.

Officer Crawley and myself accompanied Mr. Moon to his house where we found several things that aroused our suspicion. A woman's jacket was hanging in the closet. There were keys on the kitchen counter. Mr. Moon said they belonged to his wife. We also found her license in a drawer in the couple's bedroom. When questioned about this Mr. Moon said his wife probably had money on her person. We found nothing else upon searching the remainder of the premises. (See attached photographs.)

And from the interview transcripts:

Captain Sykes: What time was it again when your wife left the premises?

Abraham Moon: Must have been close to midnight.

CS: And she didn't say where she was going?

AM: No, sir. She didn't.

CS: And you didn't chase after her?

AM: She needed some time to herself. Least that's how I saw it.

CS: Mr. Moon, where was your daughter, Jessica, is it, all this time?

AM: At my mother's house. She was supposed to come back Sunday but now she's staying there until we sort this out.

CS: Did your wife ever indicate that she might be moving away?

AM: She'd threatened. I mean she talked about it. She was always talking like that.

CS: Was your wife having an affair?

AM: Yes, Captain. I believe she was.

On and on it goes. Tactful questions. Concise answers revealing nothing, except the stoic man's conviction that his wife was still alive. There was an equally unproductive interview with young Jessica, which served only to establish the girl's undying love for her stuffed panda bear.

After reading pages of interviews and studying the photographs taken when the police first searched the house, Hank learns nothing new. Abraham thought she'd be back. She had left before and stayed away for days. He only grew suspicious when she didn't make it to work on Monday. Hank has no idea what the mystery-letter writer expected him to find.

"Do you mind if I borrow this for a couple days, Dan?" he asks upon returning upstairs.

"I don't think we'll be needing them here," Dan replies. "If we do, we know where to find you."

Lindsay ceases her basketball alarm clock routine at forty-seven minutes past nine. She'd kept it up for over an hour. Will gives her high marks for endurance and persistence. He lies in bed, not at all eager to stand and rejoin the living for fear that he might pass a mirror and be forced to look at himself.

There's no explaining what has happened, what is happening. He has gone from being a caring partner in an adult relationship to being a love-struck teenager helplessly following his hormones. Thank God for the fire. Thank God he was able to get away before further damage was done.

And yet, even now, he knows he wants to see her again. He knows that if she walked through that door, he'd surrender without much resistance. Maybe it's the fact of their shared histories, abandonment, and loss. Or maybe her beauty has blinded him. Or maybe he is drawn to her sorrow, to all sorrow. Or maybe he's just a screwup, plain and simple. Whatever the case, he is reluctant to leave his single bed. It doesn't help that he hasn't had a good night's sleep in over a week. Something's got to give, he thinks, as he drags his sorry ass into the bathroom.

He expected an immediate ambush from his young co-tenant and is surprised not to find her waiting for him outside. He walks slowly out into another clear, sunny Fairmont day, wanting Lindsay to have a fair shot at him. He could use a little innocent distraction. He lingers for a moment then decides that she and her mom must have gone to the pool.

As he walks to Claire's, he tries not to think, at least not about her, or about what he will say. He knows if he thinks about this dreadful mission, he might be tempted to abort. It's not unlike his childhood approach to dentist appointments. He trained himself not to think about them until the moment he sat in the dreaded metal chair. Claire is there. He is going to see her. That's as far as he lets his mind go with it.

*

He knocks, which is sad to begin with, and looks tired when she opens the door. She wants to touch him, to hug him, but doesn't. No mixed signals. She promised herself.

"Hi," he says, waiting for her to indicate it's all right for him to enter.

"Hi," she replies, leading him to the couch, leaning her guitar against the end table as she sits.

"Ready for tonight?" he asks.

"I guess."

She doesn't want small talk. She doesn't want to allow themselves the feeling of not knowing one another any longer. They're not strangers, for God's sake. She refuses to speak until he says something meaningful. He seems to understand.

"Listen, Claire," he begins, "I don't know what to say. Something's going on with me. I'm not sure what."

"What do you mean you're not sure what?" she replies, resentment surfacing. "That's just not good enough, Will."

"I guess it started with the miscarriage. I think it freaked me out more than I realized. The commitment. The idea that we could have a baby together. I didn't even know it was happening, Claire. I started running."

"Is there another woman?" she asks, knowing the answer but needing to hear it.

"Not really," he says. "I mean, yes, but not really. Nothing serious. It just kind of happened."

"What kind of happened? Did you sleep with her?"

"No," he interjects too quickly. "Of course I didn't sleep with her. I just talked with her."

"With who?" she asks.

"Wait a second, Claire. That's not what this is really about. This isn't about another woman. I think I just need some time to sort things out. I know I still love you and that I'm being stupid. I'm just feeling a little mixed up."

She waits before speaking, choosing her words carefully.

Finally, she says, "You do what you need to do, Will, but don't expect me just to sit here waiting for you. I don't appreciate the way you've handled this so far. I don't like the way it makes me feel about myself. So ... obviously you're gonna do what you're gonna do. I just don't know for sure that I'll be here when you're done."

She sees his panic dissolve into resignation. He leans toward her opening his long arms, and she lets him hold her because that's what they do. That's how they're comfortable. But as she does, she can't help wondering if this will be the last time she finds herself on the receiving end of Will's embrace.

The theatre. The carpet store. Tom's Tuxedos. Imperial's. Stanley drives fifteen miles per hour, block after familiar block. It's the tail end of rush hour, Friday evening, a reckless and dangerous time of the week. He likes to make sure the town is secure before he goes back to his apartment for a *Columbo* double feature. Columbo is his all-time favorite television detective.

When he was a boy, being a policeman was all Stanley dreamed of—solving crimes, keeping good citizens safe. But his father told him a job like that might be a little tricky for someone like him. His father got him a simpler, more manageable job at the Iron Works instead—a job he lost when the company downsized again twelve years ago. Since then his father has made sure Stanley didn't need any job at all, sending monthly checks for rent, groceries and other expenses.

Stanley continues his nightly patrol. In a way, he thinks, he is a policeman. In these quiet moments, driving alone, he protects and serves, just like the real cops do. It helps that he is invisible. Not really, he knows, but kind of. He can walk closely behind someone and have that person not see him; he can walk so quietly that the sound of his steps goes undetected by the human ear.

He passes the bar. His big brother, Joe, is inside. Stanley sees him and all the others through the window. He wishes he could stop but knows that the bar is off limits. It's for his own good, Joe says.

"People won't understand what a special guy you are," Joe has told him. "People are cruel, Stanley. They'll make fun of you."

Stanley recalls the times long ago when people were mean to him. Joe was always there making everything okay until eventually nobody teased him any more.

At the Fulton Road stop sign, Stanley pulls his gold watch from his right front pocket. 6:15 p.m. Before making the left down to Freeport, he glances in the rearview mirror, hoping that Joe will magically appear. He knows that it's time to start watching him again.

✻

Nobody knew how happy he was. Well, Jessica maybe. But she was just a child. Beverly didn't know. He had inherited his parent's inability to say things, to translate feelings, even good ones, into words. So Beverly hadn't known how fascinating and beautiful he found her, how hearing her speak was like breathing in air, how happy she made him for most of their time together.

Abraham wonders now, all these years later, why she hadn't been more suspicious of those notes he supposedly slipped her in high school. It simply wasn't in his nature to have written them. Eventually he'd lied and told her Hank had written them for him—but that was years into their marriage. And speaking of Hank, why hadn't he blown the whistle? Abraham will never know.

The fact was Abraham would have said all of the things in those notes if he'd known how. He'd fallen in love with Beverly long before Hank did, years and years before—when they were both children.

In addition to his reputation as the area's finest hunter, Abraham's dad had come to be known as someone who could fix things. It became a kind of side job. On weekends, when he wasn't off guiding some amateur hunter through the woods of Pennsylvania, he would sometimes get calls from people needing his help, needing a handyman they could hire "off-the-books," who wouldn't charge them an arm and a leg.

When Abraham was in third grade, he accompanied his father on one such mission. There'd been a break in the water line at Miscelli's Tailor Shop, and Tasso Miscelli had called Mr. Moon to repair it. Abraham had kept his familiar station, beside and slightly behind his dad, his small hand clutching the bottom of the coat that always smelled of wood smoke. As the first-generation Italian-American shop owner explained the situation, Abraham glanced around the tiny workspace. In the corner, hunched over clothing with needles in hand, he saw the two of them, a woman and a girl. There was no doubt that they were mother and daughter, the girl was practically a miniature replica of the frowning woman on her left. As Abraham quietly studied their profiles—*her* profile—the world changed.

Though her hair was oily and her appearance plain, he saw in her a beauty that, before then, he had only glimpsed in nature; the kind that made him want to kick off his shoes and run barefoot through the woods. There weren't words for what he felt, of course, but looking back he swears it was love and that he somehow recognized her, even then, as his other half, his answered prayer, a flower growing out of life's cracked pavement.

From that day on, he knew where to find her, and would, any chance he could. As he got older and had more freedom to roam about the town, he would run to his hidden spot across from Miscelli's and post long vigils, waiting. Year after year, he had collected stolen glimpses until they formed into an image he hoped could last a lifetime.

So, of course, Abraham had taken advantage of his opportunity when it arrived in the person of Hank Shaw. He had to. He had no choice.

And Abraham never regretted his underhanded opportunism. How could he regret something that brought him the girl he'd always imagined being with? How could he regret an action that led to the birth of their beautiful baby? Yes, he had been happy, happier than anyone knew. He'd almost forgotten.

Abraham thinks of these things – of everything, really – as he sits at his table nursing his third whiskey and soda. He had to consciously fight the urge to laugh when he entered the bar over an hour ago. The way they looked at him. Their transparent fascination with the "murderer among them." He's a celebrity again.

They think he didn't read it. He's sure of that. Of course, he's worked at maintaining his appearance and keeping his transformation from their watchful eyes. Everything's changed, though. When he read those words on the heels of his daughter's mean homecoming, heard that story retold after so many years, it was like a light went on inside him, illuminating his life, inspiring him to reclaim it.

It's a struggle setting his seven dollars on the table. He wants to stay and drink and listen to the girl singer who has been setting up for the last twenty minutes. But anything out of his normal routine might alert them to the fact of his awakening. It's not time for that. Forcing a frown, he stands to leave.

"See you next time, Mr. Moon," the Camden boy says as Abraham walks toward the door.

🌰

"Can I have your attention please?" Joe calls from the makeshift stage by the window. Claire sits on a stool right behind him and waits her turn at the microphone. As Joe gives his welcome speech and pleads on behalf of the Pittsburgh Food Bank, Claire glances around the room at the familiar faces. It's a packed house. Will was working the bar when she arrived close to seven. Their eyes met for an instant. She hasn't looked at him since.

"And so, without further ado," Joe concludes, "let's hear it for the best young singer-songwriter I've come across in a long, long time, Claire Jordan!"

The audience claps politely as she begins her first song. As she breaks into the chorus, she notices a woman entering the bar—a strikingly beautiful woman, tall and thin with straight brown hair.

Claire closes her eyes and forces herself to keep singing.

Dan Finbar had arrived at Joe's and taken the table Claire had reserved for him. The tension in the air was palpable, he had observed. Will, appearing sad and distracted, worked the bar. Claire couldn't even look up. Her voice was sure on target, though, as pure and rich as any Dan ever heard. He had been unable to resist joining her for her last song, a cover of Neil Young's *Helpless*.

Now they stand in front of Joe's, having made a hasty exit after the final note.

"Sorry to rush you out of there," Claire says. "I couldn't take another second of that."

"Of what?" Fin asks.

"Of that spectacle," she replies, a scream implied in her whispered words. "Did you see her?"

Finbar had, of course, seen her. Every single man in the place had seen her, and the women, too, probably.

"Yeah," he replies, and follows her cue to start walking.

"She's so pretty," Claire observes, sadly. "I mean, she's beautiful. I almost can't blame him for falling for her."

"That's crazy," Fin reasons. "You're as pretty as she is, Claire, just in a different way. And I bet she couldn't sing her way out of a paper bag. By the way, I've been meaning to ask you something. The record company is finally coughing up the cash for a real tour, bus and everything, and I was wondering if you'd want to come out with us? Two months. You could help with Makenna and open some of the shows. I could pay you $300 a week."

Claire remains silent, though her step slows slightly.

"Did you hear me, Claire?" Fin asks.

"I heard you, Fin. Can you give me a few days to think about it?"

"We're actually heading out the middle of next week," he replies. "So the sooner you let me know, the better. Though I know it's a big decision. I think it would be fun though, Claire."

Fin's mind flashes on his morning dream. He wonders if his motives are of a purely practical nature. He forces his thoughts away from that question as the two friends continue walking.

"Care to meet me in the bathroom?" John Parker asks. He's just joined Jessica at the bar. Seats always seem to open up for people like him. Jessica isn't sure if his bathroom invitation centers on sex or drugs. Probably both.

"No thanks," she replies.

"Come on, J," he persists. John Parker has his own nicknames for everyone, even people he's just met. It all adds to his air of entitlement.

"No, JP," Jessica replies, joining him in the ranks of nicknamers. She's never called him that before.

"JP?"

"Yeah, JP. You like it?"

John ponders a moment.

"Yeah," he says. "I do. Keep calling me it, okay?"

"No problem, JP."

Jessica smiles at her spoiled sex acquaintance. He's so simple. So easy to predict and understand. All men are, really. She glances at Will behind the bar. She likes the way he looks in his faded jeans and CBGBs T-shirt. She looks forward to their next encounter. He doesn't seem quite as predictable as the others. He's definitely different.

"I can't stand any more fucking folkie music," John declares. "You want to come up to Matt's condo with me?"

"Not tonight, JP. I have other plans."

Hank Shaw drinks in the commotion surrounding him. Claire, who reminds him of a young Joni Mitchell, just finished a wonderful set, and the place is buzzing again.

"Move your ass," Donna yells at Joe over the din. Joe stands his ground but begins frenetically gyrating his hips. Donna laughs then repeats, "Move your ass, Joe."

"What do you think I'm doing?"

Hank lets his sights shift, always the reporter, always the thoughtful observer. Will pours drinks at the other end of the bar. Dominic Perchetti, looking serious and intent, listens to Larry Paul hold forth on some subject or other. Chuck Proffer tries unsuccessfully to get Ingrid Miller's attention. Dan the cop inhales a plate of wings. Jessica Moon, of all people, sits at the bar beside John Parker. Bartholomew Tucker waves his drink as he regales Raylene Jenkins with tales of his worldly travels.

These are his people. This is his world.

"Where's Claire, Joe?" Hank asks when Joe approaches for a refill. Hank needs to clarify a few song titles for his review of Claire's set.

"She left with Fin," Joe replies. "She wasn't feeling too hot, though you sure couldn't hear it in her singing. Damn, that girl can sing."

Hank nods his head in emphatic agreement and wonders why Claire left without speaking to Will. He assumes they're still a couple.

Irene Turtleman, as she had looked that day at the office, appears, uninvited, in his head. He wonders what she is doing at that very moment. Does she have a boyfriend? Hobbies? Strange, he thinks. He's never wondered such things before. And if he's not mistaken, she's looked prettier lately.

Will leans the broom against the bar and kneels to collect the gathered debris. He can't remember a more difficult night. Sadness had overtaken him the instant he heard Claire's singing, and intensified when Finbar joined her for that Neil Young cover. It hasn't lifted yet.

"You all right?" Joe asks after emerging from the office. "You look like somebody just shot your dog."

"I don't know," Will replies, suddenly exhausted beyond words.

"You need to talk?"

"No. Thanks, Joe. I just need to pop my head out of my ass before I ruin my life."

"Oh, well if that's all," Joe says, gently patting his friend's back. "Don't be too hard on yourself, man. She is beautiful."

"Am I that obvious?" Will wants to ask, but doesn't. He'd tried to keep from looking at Jessica all night, especially when Claire was still there. And Jessica seemed to take the hint. Will brought her a couple of drinks but that was the extent of their interaction. She left by herself, just before closing, offering only a smile in the way of good-bye. Will had been relieved to see her go.

"Good night," Will says, moments later, once his final chore is completed.

"You sure you don't want to talk about anything?" Joe asks again. "Sometimes it helps."

"Yeah, I'm sure," Will replies.

Will has a strange relationship with his car. His life seems to lead him away from the faithful beast, and Will often leaves it parked for days in any number of locations before suddenly finding himself beside it again and in need of its services.

He pulls open the heavy, rusted gray door and climbs in behind the giant wheel. As he turns the ignition, he hears a gentle scratching on the passenger-side window. Jessica Moon smiles down at him. He leans over and lets her in.

Before she can even say a word, Will asks, "Would you be up for spending the night in a motel?"

"Sounds good to me."

They drive together out of Fairmont.

The water is warmer than she expected.

He thought she was dead that whole time. She chokes with laughter, recalling his expression when he opened the trunk and found her wide-eyed, looking back at him. He clubbed her again and tied the cement block to her waist, cursing and berating her all the while. But still, she'd surprised him. No small feat.

The dirty water forces its way down her throat, into her stomach and lungs. "He thought I was dead," she thinks again, so proud of herself for fighting him until the bitter end.

Tricia Poe dies gracefully and feels the gentle hand of God on her weightless soul.

6

At first Stanley's disability, his mild retardation or whatever you wanted to call it, felt like a burden, a punishment, almost. But behind Martha's able, graceful leadership they all came to view it as a gift. The boy's childlike innocence didn't fade with age. The awe that overtook him as he witnessed all life's simple mysteries never went away.

And they learned to see life through Stanley's eyes. Their patience with each other and with the world at large grew with each passing day. He was their teacher. He was their gift. Martha explained all this to him again and again until finally he believed. Their love nurtured Stanley to the point that he was able to function on his own in society, no small feat.

Joe Junior was like Stanley's second father, the six-year difference in their ages seeing to that. Dozens of times, reports came home of young Joe fighting in Stanley's defense, instantly rectifying every injustice thrown upon his misunderstood little brother. Joe Junior was Stanley's protector, his guardian angel. When Joe Senior went on hunting or golfing trips, he knew he was leaving Stanley in the capable hands of both Martha and Joe.

Joe Senior's sips get larger as his thoughts shift from Stanley to Joe. He grimaces as the liquid burns its way down his throat. He drinks to pass out, to fade away, to die before the next part, before the final punishment – remembering.

Joe Junior. When Joe Junior was a little boy, looking at him had been like looking into some strange time-lapse mirror that showed you yourself forty years younger; that showed you the child you once were. It was the damnedest thing. They were the same person practically.

He thinks of all this as he drinks himself closer to oblivion. He thinks of the coward he is for being here in fucking Florida, a million miles away from them both. And just before his eyes finally close, he thinks of a phrase he learned somewhere, Sunday school probably.

Lie of omission.

*

Neither one has spoken since they got in the car. Jessica's rage is unmistakable. As he stops for the light at Fulton, Will mentally revisits their night of passion.

It began with a promise issued silently from both of them as they began their unexpected journey across the town line. The sign flashed "Vacancy" outside of Motel 3, halfway between Fairmont and Wilson. Without conversation, they pulled into the empty parking lot. By the time they reached their room, reasons for restraint had vanished like clouds into night.

He pushed her hard against the wall, and they kissed like they hadn't two nights before. Her body was warm and fluid beneath his touch, and her counter-resistance guided them onto the bed. She straddled his waist and interrupted their kiss to lift off her top. Her wild brown hair fell past her closed eyes, her smooth brown shoulders, and her slanting sides were an unambiguous arrow downward.

It was then, as he reached for the bronze button of her faded jeans that his conscience appeared, the conscience which had been on holiday for six days.

"I love Claire," were the words that popped unexpectedly from his mouth.

Will turns his head, smiling as he replays this section of the story in his mind. He doesn't mind it when the mechanical crossbars fall, protecting them from the oncoming train. He is more than happy to sit idling here in the still-dark morning.

"What?" Jessica had spit in reply to his proclamation. "The singer chick from the bar last night?"

"Yeah," he answered, nudging her gently from her perch above him. "She's my girlfriend."

"Your what?"

And so began their lopsided conversation, his end of which was brightened by the overdue breakthrough. He loved Claire. He didn't want to screw it up. He hoped beyond hope that he hadn't already.

Jessica's end, however, was not so triumphant. Her clipped, staccato responses were peppered with curses and continued topless advances. If it weren't for her vast reserve of ugly vengefulness, he might have felt sorry for her. He had misled her, after all. He'd misled them both.

Their drive continues after the train has passed. When they reach Jessica's car on Allegheny Boulevard, Will puts his in park and turns to her.

"I'm really sorry, Jessica," he says. "I don't know what I've been thinking."

She won't look at him. Her hand rests on the door handle.

"I know you don't deserve this shit," he continues, though the words are a lie. She does deserve this, a symbolic retaliation on behalf of all the men she has tormented over the years, on behalf of her poor, beaten-down father. "You're just so beautiful," he adds, as if it explains everything.

Tears fill her eyes as she glances back at him. She is clearly hurt, and he realizes that this is their first honest interaction. He's found the flesh and blood being beneath all that perfection. She leaves the car and slams the door behind her.

Will feels like walking, like breathing, like being outside. He drives up and down the town's quaint streets before parking on Jessica's, though a block away from her house so as not to be spotted. He gets out of his car and heads back to the intersection where he turns right into the Dark Hollow Hills Nature Preserve.

It's almost impossible finding Jessica's secret place, her childhood refuge. After three unsuccessful tries, he finally lunges between the correct couplet of trees and stands within the hidden enclave. The birds, the wind, the world outside are silent. Charred grass marks the spot they occupied during his previous visit.

It's not exactly praying that Will does now in this silent thatch of Fairmont Forest. It's more a form of meditation. He breathes in the air and lets his mind float freely. Not forcing thought. Not forcing anything.

Claire hovers on the wind, and at the tip of each soft, fragile, sunlight beam. He'll go to her this morning. He'll supply her with every last detail of his misspent week. He'll plead for her forgiveness and trust. He wonders what she'll say. Last night she was more distant than he would ever have imagined she could be. He winces at the changes he inspired.

"Howdy," says the man with the gray and black crew cut. Abraham Moon.

Startled to momentary breathlessness, Will manages to reply with a reluctant "Hey."

He considers his situation. He is trapped in an enclosed, little-known area with a man who may have murdered his wife. A man who might feel justified in leading Will to a similar fate for penning the words that breathed life back into a story he had wanted to remain buried. A man who is taller than Will would have thought—easily six feet. Broader, too. Kind of handsome, come to think of it.

"Saw you walking. Thought I'd say hello."

What's that supposed to mean, Will wonders? He feels like some inanimate object has sprung to life before him. Not a burning bush, exactly. More like a talking boulder.

"Jessica told me about this spot," Will replies, forcing a calm he doesn't feel, certain the instant the words leave his mouth that this will be Abraham's call to violence. Instead, the older man grunts.

"Just thought I'd say hello," Abraham repeats then leaves as quickly and quietly as he arrived.

Abraham emerges from the clearing and continues down Beech trail until he finds the small lake that is the unofficial border of Fairmont. He stares, smiling at the water's glassy sheen, pleased with the terror he witnessed in the young bartender. The golden dawn reminds him of another long ago.

They'd graduated high school the week before and had begun to work their jobs full time. Friday night, June 17, they drove together up to Wilson where they met Beverly's mom and Abraham's parents in the courthouse foyer. They'd all dressed in their Sunday best–which for Abraham meant the stiff black pants and jacket he'd inherited from his father. Like a roughly groomed herd, they walked up the steps to the wedding room where a stuttering Justice of the Peace united them in matrimony. Awkward embraces followed, and the happy couple proceeded to drive four hours to Bear Rocks, Maryland, where they settled into Cabin #4.

The next day, the day he remembers now, was the one more perfect than any other. He'd awakened her with kisses down her spine and they made love with a passion they hadn't been able to muster the night before. He brought her breakfast in bed, and they made love again before dressing for the day.

They walked to the stables where Abraham talked horses with the old man who rented them his two best Palominos. They rode at a trot until they found the open country and began to canter. Beverly laughed as the speed increased.

"Abe," she squealed. "Wait up. I don't know what I'm doing."

He circled back then took off away from her again. This time she followed. They stopped at a creek bed and watched their horses nose at the brown water. She told him they reminded her of the way he ate. He gently punched her arm and nearly knocked her from her saddle.

That evening, they dined in a large country inn. Staring across the table, he struggled to find the words that were so foreign to him. He wanted to express the fact that the day had been the best one of his life, that she had brought him happiness he'd never imagined possible. He wanted to gush his affection and awe and describe the way he perceived her: perfect and beautiful. For the first time in his life, he regretted the silence with which his parents had surrounded him. He regretted his inability to converse as the rest of the world did.

After they finished and the bill had been settled, he took her hand and stammered, "I'll love you 'til I die, Beverly."

For too many years, he's made good on his promise.

<hr/>

Dominic sits in the breakfast nook he and Maria had shared each morning. He hasn't slept. The awakening of the ancient scandal has served to bring long-buried memories to the surface. He sees it all as if it happened yesterday, not twenty years ago: his wild, hungry mornings with Beverly, the conversations afterward that got more and more loaded with significance.

"I want you to take me away from here, Dominic," she purred, her head resting on his chest. "I'm so tired of this place … of Abraham. I don't think I can handle one more day of silence."

In those moments, still drunk from the lust she'd inspired, then siphoned, he'd give her the answer she wanted.

"Soon," he'd say. "I just need to get a few more things in order." He'd banish the thoughts of his other love, his truer love, and of the daughter whose welfare Beverly didn't seem to consider. "Soon," he'd say again before rising to dress.

Though it's barely light out, returning to sleep is not an option. Hank feels the same restless energy he felt all those years ago. He is the town's lone soldier of truth. The responsibility to put this case to bed, once and for all, rests firmly on his shoulders. He will not truly rest until his mission is accomplished.

He showers and dresses, pondering the difference between now and then. Now he has that most elusive, yet necessary, of ingredients, coveted and sought by all great reporters: a source, anonymous so far, but still, a source. His own Deep Throat.

It's almost nine o'clock when he reaches the office, quiet on a Saturday morning. A few days before, it had been no more than the base for his realty business but now it is Command Central, and will remain that until the case is cracked. Articles, police reports and Polaroid photographs are strewn across the giant layout desk. He stands and stares, wondering for the hundredth time what the devil he's supposed to be discovering. And yet, there's something here. He can sense it.

He remembers life in Fairmont when Beverly was still alive and married to Abraham. It had been hard, living in the same small town with them, seeing them every couple of weeks, walking to church or dropping Jessica at her grandparents' house, which was not far from his. Beverly's beauty only blossomed and grew more striking through the years, and he couldn't shake his sense that her love was a prize meant for him, not that ignorant oaf.

How could she have thought Abraham had written those inspired poems? Surely time had shown her the impossibility of that. He held out hope that one day it would dawn on her–*everything*. Not only the fact that the man she called her husband was an imposter–a plagiarist of sorts–but also, she'd remember the shy boy whose kindred spirit she had sensed through the long, lonely days of high school, and know it was he, Hank Shaw, who had actually won her heart.

He would have welcomed her and her sullen little daughter, too. He would have been overjoyed to forgive and forget and call them his family.

His thoughts are disrupted by the phone's brittle ring. He picks up the receiver and hears a deep, muffled, indistinguishable voice say, "Follow the trail. X marks the spot. I'll call again tomorrow morning."

As Hank returns the phone to its cradle, he smiles at his own cool calm.

Morrison's farm is seven miles north of Fairmont. Jessica drives there Saturday morning in John Parker's sleek, black Corvette. Will's closing comment still stings. He'd acted as if her beauty was some barely navigable obstacle course, a test for him to endure – one he ultimately passed. Pulling down the familiar, if nearly forgotten, dirt and gravel driveway, she wonders if he is closer to the truth than she cares to admit.

"Oh my God," yells a tall, thin, gray-haired man as he carries a dirty yellow cube of hay from the backyard to the stable. "Jessica Moon. Is that you?"

When Jessica was seven, her father and Mr. Morrison had begun their barter system: hunting expeditions for Mr. Morrison, horse-back riding lessons for young Jessica. By the time Jessica was ten, she was riding every weekend and doing odd jobs around the farm for the Morrisons. They became her surrogate parents.

"In the flesh," she answers, walking from the car. "How's it going, Mr. Morrison?"

"I think you're old enough to call me Tim now," the smiling old man replies then yells, "Get out here, Holly. We have a visitor."

Jessica is surprised by the joy she feels as Mrs. Morrison emerges from the house. She hadn't known how badly she missed the kind woman.

"Jessica," she calls, breaking into a jog. "My, my, my. Didn't you turn into a beauty."

"Thank you, ma'm," Jessica replies with a politeness she hasn't employed in years. "It's really good to see you."

She hugs them both and provides them with the Reader's Digest version of her life, apologizing for disappearing like she did she when she hit her teens and revealing her hidden agenda for being there.

"Think I could take a horse out for a while?" she asks shyly. "I haven't ridden in forever and could really use it."

The beaming couple step over each other to grant the young girl's simple request.

"Dusty?" Jessica asks hopefully.

"You got it," Mrs. Morrison answers. Dusty was the horse Jessica first learned on. He was easily the best friend she ever had, aside from her stuffed panda doll. "He'll be overjoyed to see you."

The sky bleeds red on the swaying, bruised tree line. Cardinals and blue jays sing loudly, their songs competing for the wide-open airwaves. The wind on her face is the fluttering of angels' wings, the touch of a trusted lover.

Jessica had not ridden horses once during her time in Nashville. She hadn't done anything that might remind her of home, of her father, of her mother, of the girl she used to be. Her vow of isolation remained firmly intact as she ricocheted through part-time jobs and cocaine cocktail parties, carelessly acquiring then discarding a string of pretty-boys. She started with the studly upperclassmen at Vanderbilt then graduated to record company execs and rising young country stars. But none of them ever had a chance.

You can get used to anything. That's what Jessica thinks out here in this place of beauty, this place that gave her so much joy and peace all those years ago. She is reminded of what she assumes she is still capable of feeling: happiness. But the years have turned her cold, and she can barely even make out the figure of that quiet but happy little girl walking to school with her father. A million years ago. You can get used to anything.

With the lower half of her body, she guides Dusty up a hill and into the farm's most spacious clearing, a dozen football fields in length at least. She's been careful not to push the old boy but doesn't restrain him as he surges into an all-out gallop. The feeling is magic, poetry in motion as he hits his stride. Jessica could swear the graceful animal is floating above the ground. It's effortless and exhilarating, absolute perfection.

Why did she let this all go, she wonders as they soar? Why had she stopped considering herself worthy of this joy, or this joy worthy of her time? How could she have denied herself this feeling for so long?

For one moment, she almost forgets all she had grown used to and becomes, again, the child she once was.

Will feels no dread as he ascends the stairs to Claire's apartment. He is happier than he's been in a long time, in fact, and anxious to share his breakthrough, his clarity. When she doesn't answer he remembers Saturday morning Yoga and her movie date with Lindsay and decides to let himself in and leave a note.

He finds a message pad and scrawls, "I love you, Claire. I'm so sorry. We need to talk. I need to talk. Call me as soon as you see this. Will." He tapes the page to the front door and leaves.

Not wanting to thwart his mood by going to his apartment, Will decides to swing by Hank's office to peruse the article he intended for last week's edition and make sure it holds up. Or maybe he should write an apology for the Moon fiasco. He's surprised when he gets there to find Hank hard at work.

"Hey, Hank," Will says, realizing that harboring a resentment against Hank Shaw would be pointless and unproductive, not to mention unnoticed.

"Hey, pal," Hank replies quickly, more agitated than usual.

Will joins him at the drawing board, as Hank likes to call it, and looks down at the spread of Moon information.

"What's all this, Hank?" he asks, weariness in his voice. "Don't you think we should just let this one go away again? It seems to stir things up in kind of a negative way."

One by one, Will picks up the photos taken of the various rooms inside the Moon house on the day Abraham reported Beverly missing. Each room looks surprisingly unspectacular. He's not sure what he expected. A chalk-marked body? A bloodstain on the wall?

Hank replies with some type of clucking noise, which seems to emanate from deep in his throat.

"I'm just going to snoop around a little more, son," he retorts. "If nothing turns up, I'll let it go for good. Promise."

As Will heads for the door Hank stops him, saying, "It's a heck of a story though, Will. One heck of a story."

"I was wondering if you'd want to come out with us? Two months. You could watch Makenna and open some of the shows. I could pay you $300 a week."

Finbar's words play over and over in Claire's head as she walks up to Lindsay's. She resists the urge to go upstairs and talk with Will.

"Hi, Claire," Lindsay says, jogging out onto the sidewalk.

It has become their policy to attend the first Saturday matinee whenever a new children's feature comes to the Guthrie.

"Hi, Lin," Claire replies cheerfully. She is always overjoyed to see Lindsay, who is the spitting image of Claire's seven-year-old self. Freckle-faced tomboy. Unrehearsed smile. The two embrace each other tightly. "Where'd you get the snazzy outfit?"

"My mom," Lindsay states, happy that Claire noticed the new ensemble.

"You like it, Claire?" Lindsay's mom calls from a second-floor window.

"Hi, Mrs. Ramsay. I love it."

"Thanks so much for doing this, Claire. Lindsay's been talking about it all week."

"My pleasure," Claire reassures. "Ready to go, Lin?"

The two wave goodbye to Lindsay's mom and walk out onto the Sixth Street sidewalk.

"Is Will working at your place?" Lindsay asks. "He never came home last night."

Claire is relieved. Her decision has practically been made for her.

"Do you mind if we make one stop on our way to the movies, Lin? I need to talk to somebody for a second. We won't be late for the movie, I promise."

Finbar is continually amazed at the richness of the time he spends with his daughter, Makenna. He prefers her company to anyone's in the world, hands-down, though they have yet to exchange words.

During his "lost time" as he now refers to it, Finbar typed out the story of his and Maggie's strange courtship years ago at Harrison College. Their mutual friend, Ransom Seaborn, had committed suicide, and the two were left to find some meaning in their loss. Night after night, they'd meet and wade through the journal that held all of Ransom's secrets. In the process, the sad survivors fell in love.

Finbar's recounting of the Ransom saga was originally going to be a suicide note of his own but has now become a symbol of mercy to him, a reminder of the unexpected epiphany that found him there in his place of despair. In lieu of therapy, he reads passages to Makenna each morning as they ease into the day. He just finished the part where he drunkenly insulted Maggie outside of her dorm and staggered off into the night. Makenna gurgles a smiling reply and Finbar laughs. It's only recently that Finbar has been able to laugh again.

The ringing of the doorbell interrupts the tender moment. Fin leaves his daughter smiling in her bouncy seat and runs to the door. Claire stands there looking just a little less distraught than she had the night before. A young girl stands beside her.

"Just the woman I wanted to see," Fin says. "Who's your friend?"

"Dan Finbar, this is Lindsay Ramsay, one of my very favorite people," Claire replies cheerfully.

The girl beams with Claire's pronouncement and timidly accepts Finbar's outstretched hand.

"Hi, Lindsay. How's it going?"

"We're heading to a movie, Fin," Claire interjects. "I just wanted to tell you that I thought about your offer, and I accept. This is the perfect time for me to get away for a while."

"Are you sure?" he asks.

"I'm sure. I really appreciate you giving me the opportunity, Fin. Was there something else you wanted?"

Fin knows that Claire had not intended this question to be loaded, but he feels a weight there, hanging in the air between them, that had not been there before she appeared in his dream. He wonders if she feels it too.

"Actually, I just found out that my sister can't watch Makenna tonight; her daughter's sick and I have a show in West Virginia and won't be home until super late. I wondered if you could babysit overnight?"

"No problem," Claire says. "Having stuff to keep me occupied is a good thing right about now. I'll come right over after the movie. Around three, okay?"

"Perfect, Claire. Thanks," Fin replies. "You're a lifesaver."

The clear summer day invigorates Hank. He breathes the warm air deeply as he walks to his car. The drive to the Moon house takes three minutes, enough time for him to formulate a strategy. He'll enter Black Hollow Hills Preserve posing as a nature lover out for a casual stroll. He grabs the binoculars he always keeps in his glove box (a true birdwatcher is always prepared) to assist in the ruse.

Slowly, stopping often to feign admiration for some flower or weed, Hank moves farther into the forest. When he is certain he's in no one's sight, he darts off the path and pauses, briefly, behind the cover of a berry bush. It's then he notices a small red cloth attached to the branch of a Maple tree farther off the path, closer to the Moon property. As he approaches it, he sees another red marker deeper within, then another. The trail ends at a thick stand of Evergreens, at least a dozen in a tight, bushy row. After several painful failed attempts to penetrate the green mass, Hank surges at last into a small, perfectly hidden clearing. A charred line marks the dirt, along with the final thin strip of red. Hank kneels reverently on what he is sure is Beverly Moon's final resting place.

Though discovering the remains of Beverly Moon would be no small accomplishment, his instincts tell him to wait one more day to alert the police. He'll have more than just a burial site to turn over—he'll have a murderer.

*

Dressed in her powder-pink jogging suit, Irene Turtleman impulsively turns her K Car into the Giant Eagle parking lot moments after she sees Mr. Shaw driving in the opposite direction. Before she can stop herself, she is following him, like one of Charlie's Angels.

She keeps her distance and reassures herself that she is doing this because he's been acting so strangely. She wants to be sure he's not getting himself into some kind of trouble. Besides, Dr. Phil says that it's healthy to get out of your "comfort zone" sometimes.

He parks on Tenth and she does too. Her heart pounds as she walks, far behind him, into the nature trail she's heard about for years, yet never visited. It is a day for firsts.

Could it really be this innocent, she thinks from behind the tree she hopes conceals her? Is he simply out enjoying nature? Is he eating that flower? No. Just studying. He is so inquisitive. She loves that about him.

She nearly faints when he looks up the pathway in her direction. She ducks farther into her hiding place then forces herself to count to sixty before taking another look. Squinting, taking tentative steps down the dirt trail, she wonders where in the heck he could have gone.

She's tempted to call for him but comes to her senses and slinks away.

✤

He hasn't thought it all the way through just yet. Abraham only knows that it feels good to be in motion, to have wheels turning and to sense the freight train gaining speed. He has owed Hank for years now. This will be the payback.

Hank. Poor Hank. Though Abraham never regretted his under-handed maneuvering at the start of his courtship with Beverly, he couldn't help feeling sorry for Hank, with whom Abraham sympa-thized. They had both been outsiders, afraid to talk. They had both loved the same woman. Abraham doubted very much that Beverly would have treated Hank kindly had the rendezvous gone as the shy poet had hoped, so in a way Abraham had spared Hank the bit-ter pain of rejection.

It was the hunter in him that had prevailed back then. The same part of his brain that knew exactly when a perfectly still twelve-point buck would run had alerted him to the fact of Hank's longing. With quiet focus, he had watched Hank stash the messages, memorized Beverly's lock combination and the love notes before she did, he had watched as the strange dance progressed, knowing each move before Hank made it. Just be there first. That was his plan the night of the dance and it couldn't have gone more perfectly.

Abraham had wanted his quarry, plain and simple. He feels that way now for the first time in years. Only the quarry is no longer the beautiful young woman, Beverly Moon. Now, the quarry is her ghost.

✤

The Pirates are surging. Three runs in the bottom of the seventh, and they've reclaimed the lead. Tyler and Joe stand cheering as another run crosses the plate.

"Looks like they might get one here, T," Joe exclaims as the two slap hands.

"It's about time," Tyler replies. The team is in the midst of yet another losing streak.

After retaking their seats, Tyler asks, "We meeting up with Tricia after the game, Dad?"

Though at first Joe's only son was reluctant to accept a new woman into their lives, the mistrust has long since transformed into friendship, with maybe a trace of infatuation.

Joe hesitates before replying. "Tricia and I are taking some time off, T. She went back to California for a while."

"Are you okay, dad?"

The question takes Joe's breath away. That the boy would be more concerned about his father's welfare than anything else strikes Joe as plain beautiful.

"Yeah, I'm okay. We just weren't really happy together anymore. So we're taking some time to figure things out." He pauses, then adds, "And sometimes you still love someone but stop being in love with them."

"Like you and mom?" Tyler asks.

Joe can't remember when Tyler's brand of conversation shifted from child to adult, but it definitely has. "Yeah, like me and mom."

"Well, whatever happens is okay with me," Tyler says.

Joe turns to wipe a prideful tear from his eye. "How'd I end up with such an amazing kid?" he asks the general PNC Park baseball-watching population. "I love you, Tyler."

"I love you too, dad."

Will and Donna are hosting the usual crew when Joe arrives at the bar through the rear entrance. He peeks into the main room but rather than saying hello, ducks straight into the office. He's feeling stressed and needs to blow off some steam.

He draws the blind and boots up. Blood pumps to all the right places. There is a vast cache of folders hidden on his computer desktop. No one would ever know it was there, and even if they did, they would be unable to access it without the password that only Joe knows, will ever know.

Hmmm. Who shall it be today: Susie from Nashville, Emma from Philadelphia, Tessa from DC–the trip where he found Will Jameson? He takes pictures every time for just this purpose, reliving the memories. Yeah. Tessa's the one. What a sweetheart.

Will barges in just as Joe is refastening his belt.

"Jesus, Will," Joe blurts. "Doesn't anyone ever knock around here?"

"Whoa, Joe," Will replies. "I didn't think you were here. We need ones."

"I spilled coffee on my jeans and had to change," Joe explains in his funny friend-voice, always quick on his feet in these types of situations. "I'll be right out with the cash."

"Joe," his friends yell in ragtag chorus, the cast of *Cheers* on Valium, when he emerges.

"Hey everybody," Joe honks in reply. When he reaches the back of the bar, he grabs a spoon and taps on the rim of the nearest glass to alert everyone to a pending announcement. With trademark sarcastic sincerity he says, "I love you all like family." Groans all around. "And because you're all like family, I wanted you to hear this from me first." The chatter dies as the group senses at least a small degree of seriousness in their friend. "Tricia and I called it quits. She left this morning. She's driving back to California."

"Are you okay, Joe?" asks Donna.

"Yeah, I'm okay. We've been struggling for a while, and I think she'll be happier out there. At least I hope she will be."

It's funny how real a lie can feel, how swept up Joe can get in his own illusions. In that moment, he cares more for Tricia than he ever has before, and his tears of concern for her growth and well-being, tears that form easily in his sad brown eyes, are almost genuine.

"So it's all for the best?" Will asks his adopted big brother.

"Yeah, it's all for the best," Joe replies, wondering silently how his young friend's ego will survive the loss of its biggest inflator.

Jessica lies on her bed and stares out the window. The sunlight fades from gold to red to blue. She's been lying here since returning from Morrison's, staring off at nothing. It's been so long since she felt this way, felt a deep despondence caused by someone else. It was after her mother left.

They're all kind of cloudy, those memories. She'd been stashed at her grandmother's, shielded from the neighbors and the media, but she knew something had been lost, and her days and nights were filled with feeling that loss, living inside of it, claiming responsibility from behind the clouds in her head.

She had known then what her mother didn't–that her dad loved them both with a fierceness he could never express, a fierceness that somehow added to the distance between them all. That was the time he talked more than ever before or since, telling her over and over, whispering it into her ear again and again, "Mommy left us, baby, but it wasn't your fault. It wasn't anybody's fault."

Why is she doing this? Why is she remembering what she's worked so hard to forget? What is happening to her?

And then the other unwanted train of thought pulls into the station. This one from a little later, when she was older but still just a girl. Her dad would take Joe Camden's dad hunting; Joe would watch Jessica while they were away. It was no big deal for him; *of course* he'd keep an eye on her; always happy to help. He was so trusted and well liked by everybody.

And it was a different time, back then.

At first his attention had felt good, like warm sunshine after years in the dark. He was funny and treated her like she was older than she was. He was the first man to ever call her beautiful.

She felt it turn, the tone of his compliments as his voice lost its breath, but she was already under his spell, too starved for attention, affection and love, to do anything other than what he asked of her, what he said was natural and okay, what he made her swear never to mention to another living soul.

She was only eleven years old.

*

Martha idolized her younger brother, Kenny. He was the golden child in the Reardon family, the one who could do no wrong. Her parents and sisters were of the same opinion but with Martha it went deeper. Joe was almost jealous of his wife's adoration but stopped short of envy because he shared in the admiration.

What wasn't to admire? The guy could throw a pigskin the length of a football field, shoot a deer at impossible distances, tell a joke like Bob Hope. He was a man's man that everybody liked being around – one of those special people.

Kenny Reardon. Martha's brother. On days when Joe is this hungover, he skips the good parts, along with his morning walk and his midday swim, and cuts straight to Kenny. He pictures them all laughing and drinking at the bar or the fire hall. He remembers the way Martha came to her only brother's defense if ever there was the slightest indication that he might be human, capable of mistakes.

And always it's the same questions he asks himself: How could his love for one person have blinded him to his love for another? How could he have allowed a bad decision to become the cornerstone of his existence? Why hasn't the cancer they promised would kill him done its job yet?

*

A perfect day. The movie had been really funny. And Claire had laughed as much as Lindsay. Lindsay loved that – hearing Claire laugh. And they'd both laughed a bunch more eating ice cream after. Claire and Lindsay, laughing and talking.

Of course, she'd been very sad to hear of Claire's plans to leave Fairmont for a while but had been comforted by her older friend's assurances that she'd receive daily reports from the road and that Claire would return bearing gifts. Claire even said that maybe some day the two of them could have an adventure like that. A "road trip." That's what Claire called it.

And she'd even had fun tonight with her mom and Phil. They made popcorn and played a kid's version of Monopoly, and Lindsay won. She really won. It wasn't just them letting her win. She outsmarted them both and got all their money and their property and everything.

A perfect day.

Just what she needed to push out the scary feeling she's been carrying, to wipe the fuzzy picture from her brain. Maybe tonight she'll finally sleep.

A stakeout. That's what they call it. Stanley is doing one on his brother. He sits in his car drinking chocolate milk, eyes glued to the bar's front door. He's pretty sure Joe won't come out before closing, but his big brother has surprised him before. Expect the unexpected. All good cops know that. It's one of the golden rules.

Mostly, he's been perfect. His only mistake so far was falling asleep outside of Joe and Tricia's last night. He wouldn't let that happen again.

Stanley remembers his friend, Lorena. They were students together at Traxel, the special school Stanley attended years ago when he had just started his teens and Joe was almost finished with his. Joe would usually drop him off and pick him up.

Lorena was in Stanley's class and was just like him–slow, but smart in other ways. She was funny and nice. Stanley liked her a lot.

As the year went on, Stanley noticed that Joe would show up

earlier and earlier and talk with Lorena while Stanley finished his work.

"She's too young for you, Joe," Stanley stammered one day on the drive home. "You talk to her too much."

"Ah, come down from your high horse," Joe had answered. "They can never be too young."

One day Stanley looked up from his notebook and saw that Joe and Lorena weren't standing where they usually stood, where they were standing two minutes before. He walked outside, an amateur detective already, and listened for their voices. He heard engines and bird whistles but no voices.

But then he knew. The car. That was where they were. Stanley ran as fast he could and got there just in time. Stanley knew the law. He knew what Joe would be if he kept touching Lorena the way he was. Stanley knew.

Afterwards, Joe had been as mad as Stanley had ever seen him, or ever has since.

"You just don't understand me, Stanley," Joe said, in a new voice, a mean one. "And if you ever interfere with my business again, I'll tell dad to ship you off to some kind of mental institution. Got that?"

Stanley nodded, not liking the feeling that came with making Joe angry.

Then it dissolved. The mad face. The mean voice.

"I love you, Stanley," Joe said next.

"I love you too, Joe."

Stanley hopes he never sees the mean Joe again.

7

"What happened to you in the past twenty-four hours?" Joe asks Will, emerging momentarily from his Tricia funk. "You're positively beaming."

"Nothing happened."

"Ve have vays of making you talk," Joe replies in a bad Nazi interrogator voice.

"I mean it, man. Nothing happened. That's what's so good. I almost hooked up with Jessica last night, thereby officially ruining my life, but I finally woke up and realized that Claire is the one I want to be spending all my nights with. I saw the freaking light!"

"How very romantic," Donna interjects, grabbing her drink order.

"I never really felt that with Tricia," Joe admits. "I wish I felt that way about somebody. You're lucky. You know that? You are lucky, my friend."

"We won't really know if that's true until I talk with Claire. I haven't been able to track her down."

"Why don't you just take off, Will," Joe suggests. "Donna and I can man the fort. Things are kind of slowing down here anyway. Go find Claire."

"You sure?"

"Hell yes, I'm sure. Go make things right with your woman."

It's another perfect night–clear, cool and breezy. The moment Will steps into it, he grabs his cell phone from the front pocket of his jeans and calls Claire at her apartment. No answer. He tries her cell. Again, no answer. Will leaves messages both places and starts walking.

Rather than over-preparing for his imminent love summit, he nudges his thoughts past Claire, to Jessica. Not Jessica the girl who almost steered him off course with her charms, but Jessica who, as a little girl, was robbed of a childhood by an unfeeling woman, a non-speaking man and a dark cloud of mystery.

As he walks, he notices a light on in Joe's car. Knowing the door will be unlocked he opens it and leans in to correct the situation, hopefully saving his friend's battery. He spots a wallet on the passenger-side floor and picks it up. Flipping it open, he's sees Tricia Poe's frowning face staring up at him from a laminated license. He considers running back in to tell Joe, but the notion is interrupted by the sound of his name.

"Will," Dominic Perchetti calls again from the bus shelter bench where he sits.

Will crosses the street and joins him there.

"Hey, Dom. Waiting for a bus? "

"I have a bad feeling," the old man says, dismissing pleasantries. "I've had a bad feeling ever since this Moon stuff came back up, Will. I know you didn't mean for that article to be printed, but, well, it's just a bad thing. That's all."

Will remains silent, sensing Dom's need to talk.

"You weren't here, then, Will. You don't know what it did to this town. This place was pretty innocent before then. People felt safe. Felt like they knew who everybody was, what everybody was. After that, no one knew anything."

A car passes. A group of teenagers laughs in the Laundromat parking lot.

"Can you make me a promise, Will?"

"Sure, Dom."

"Can you promise me you won't write one more word about Abraham or Beverly Moon? We need to let that dog go back to sleep."

"I'm not the one you need to talk to, Dom. Hank seems intent on keeping the story alive. I tried to get him to let it go, but he just wasn't hearing it."

"Hank." Dominic shrugs. "That man's been in over his head since the day he was born. Well, whatever happens, will happen," he observes with resignation. "Just promise me you won't throw any more fuel on the fire? Can you do that for me?"

"It's already done." Will assures and stands to leave.

It's been a long, full day. After the movie and a stop at the ice cream parlor, Claire walked Lindsay home and headed straight for Fin's. She's somehow managed to keep her thoughts from Will, focusing instead on the invitation she's accepted and on the baby she's been watching all evening.

Maggie's smile casts light from a square, silver frame. Maggie. Finbar's wife. Claire reflects on the fact that the pictured young woman, the mother of the baby sleeping in the next room, can smile no more. How can that be? How could a smile as alive as the one captured here be taken from the world so abruptly?

And why did Claire's baby die when others thrive under far worse circumstances? Is there a force beyond making these harsh, seemingly random choices on humanity's behalf? If so, does this force give a rat's ass for anyone's happiness? Could there really be some meaning behind it all: cosmic lessons for us dim-witted humans to puzzle over?

A buzzing from Claire's purse interrupts her dark thoughts on life's fundamental unfairness. She reaches in to retrieve her phone. "Missed Call" reads the message on the tiny screen. She doesn't have to check. She knows it was Will. He must have tried her when she was putting Makenna down. Without giving herself the chance to hesitate, she calls him back.

"What?" she asks his breathless voice.

"Where are you?"

She's annoyed. He is not allowed to ask where she is, or to expect anything of her, even a simple answer. He no longer has any rights where she is concerned.

"What the hell do you care?" she snaps, the pent-up hostility beginning to breathe.

"I just wondered if you'd been by your place," he replies. "I left you a note. I really need to talk to you, Claire."

"Well, now's not a good time," she says. "I'm at Finbar's watching Makenna all night, and I just don't feel like going into all this. And I don't think a little note from the novelist is going to make everything okay."

"Wait, Claire," he says before she can disconnect. "Can you just give me two minutes?"

She sits and nods, braces herself, waits.

"Claire, I can't believe what a jerk I've been," he begins. "And I'll totally understand if you can't get past this. But I need you to know that I love you, and I realize that you're the only one I want to be with. I think the baby and the loss of the baby were just too much for me to compute, so I freaked, and I ran. But I realize now that there's no one to run to who could ever give me more than you do. You're my best friend and the person I want to spend my life with, and I'll do anything to make you realize how much I mean it."

She's quiet. She hears the tears forming in his words. There's a part of her drinking it in, as thirsty for this as she's ever been for anything in her entire life. It's the unquenched damaged part that speaks, though.

"Why the hell should I believe you, Will? And even if I did, how do I know you won't freak out anytime any kind of stress comes our way? I just don't know if I can trust you. I feel like you showed your true colors and you'll show them again. Like maybe it's just inevitable." She pauses, waiting for the exact right thought. "I think I've lost my faith in you."

Back and forth they go. He understands, he says, but he knows the past week was an aberration. He tells her everything. More, maybe, than she even wants to hear. His direct honesty begins to wear down her defenses. After a densely-packed hour has flown by, her harshness has evolved into fatigue.

"I can't think about all this anymore tonight, Will. I need some time."

After agreeing to talk more the next day, she closes her phone and collapses onto Finbar's couch.

The Miracle Lanes Bowling Alley is a throwback to another time with its gaudy abundance of visual stimuli, its pink and brown color scheme, its unique two-story architecture–arcade on the second floor, bowling lanes on the first. Tonight it is packed, as it is every Saturday night. Hank has a standing reservation for lane twelve–his lucky number. He spits on his trusty blue bowling shoes then brushes them to a sparkling shine. This is his medicine, his lone escape from the stresses of his life.

Hank will admit that some nights he envies the groups he encounters there, the laughing families and boisterous bands of friends. He envies their togetherness as he bowls alone; their jovial roughhousing between frames. This is not the case tonight, however. He is grateful for his status as a lone wolf. For even though he appears to be focused on his form and delivery, his mind is still scanning the facts of the Moon case. Something is gnawing at the murky depths of his subconscious. He can't say what. It runs again now, the highlight reel in his head: his old articles, the "crime scene" pictures, the police interviews, the hidden grave site. What is he missing?

"Oh well, there can't be much more," he surmises. "Soon I'll know everything."

He is already planning the all-night work session, preparing the *Reporter's* first special edition in twenty years. Irene will be with him, reading his mind, meeting each unspoken need. Who knows, maybe Will can even help bring the thing home.

He already knows what the front-page headline will read:

Moon Case Solved After 20 Years

Only now Hank will be more than just the messenger. He will also be a key player, the man who cracked the case. And that's exactly how he will be remembered. His legacy will be secured.

As his heart races with the daydream, he is surprised to see Irene Turtleman, looking quite fetching in a thin blue turtleneck, enter through the front door with a group of girlfriends. Not a man among them. Why had that been the first thing he noticed? And why couldn't he seem to look away from her now? Had she chosen Miracle Lanes for her Saturday night outing because she knew Hank would be here? Was she looking back at him now?

Emboldened, perhaps, by the exhilarating roller-coaster ride his life has become over the past few days, he walks the three lanes over to her. He is relieved when she moves from her group to meet him in the spectator area.

"Hi, Mr. Shaw," she says with a smile he hasn't seen from her before–a Saturday-night smile.

"Call me Hank," he implores. "We're not in the office after all. I had no idea you bowled, Irene."

"First time," she confesses.

"Well would your friends mind if you joined me for a few frames?" he asks, surprised, himself with his recklessness. "I could teach you the basics."

"They wouldn't mind at all," she replies without even a moment's hesitation. "Just let me get my purse."

She retrieves her modest brown handbag and bids adieu to her stunned comrades. Over the next two hours Hank uses his reporting skills to learn about Irene, something he should have done years ago. He's not sure why he hasn't. She has always just been so shy.

Her father was an itinerant preacher who roamed the hills and hidden country of West Virginia, spreading the gospel. Irene spent her childhood roaming with him, accompanied by her rambunctious younger brother and her meek, obedient mom.

"I have to admit it was kind of a hard childhood," she says after completing the first exhilarating spare of her life. "He was a little crazy and a little heavy on the fire and brimstone. I think that's why we were all so shy. His personality was big enough for the whole family.

"I'm not complaining," she was quick to add. "He was who he was. I'm sure he had his reasons. A lot of people are a lot worse off than we were."

The paragraphs that continue to pour forth from between Irene's thin lips, paragraphs about bird watching and Oprah Winfrey and the wonderful climate in Fairmont this time of year, distract Hank from all he's had on his mind. They talk and they bowl, and he is reminded of how good he felt running to meet Beverly that night long ago … before the heartbreak.

"So this is how it feels," he thinks. "I'll be damned."

It was always on the nights after the concerts. Joe would insist they stay a day or two longer to make it more of a vacation. The two brothers would sit on their double beds, talking over delivered pizza and watching TV like the nights before. But some time after the lights were out, Joe would creep from his bed to the bathroom, dress and slip from the room as Stanley pretended to sleep.

The first few years he just waited there replaying detective shows in his mind. That was the trick he used to help himself fall to sleep. It usually worked and Stanley wouldn't remember his brother's return, and neither one would mention anything about it the next day.

The fourth year, though, when Stanley was 20 and Joe was 26, instead of remaining in bed and conjuring up old police shows, Stanley got up and dressed quickly, hoping to test out his sleuthing skills and follow his brother on his secret excursion. They were in Charlottesville, Virginia that year.

Joe always walked, a good thing for Stanley who would have been unable to follow if his brother had taken the car. The first thing that struck Stanley that night was the strange clothes Joe wore–clothes Stanley never saw before, at least not on his brother. Stanley stayed hidden a safe distance behind as Joe sauntered down Main Street and took a seat on a bench outside of a hamburger joint called "Charlie's."

Eventually a cute young girl stepped out of the diner, and Joe said something to her as she walked by him to use a nearby pay phone. After her call, she paused again at Joe's bench, but remained this time, the two settling into conversation. Stanley observed the way the girl laughed, the way she swayed as she talked, nervously twirling her long brown hair. Stanley guessed she was fourteen.

Stanley left then, choosing not to observe any further. His brother was probably just dressed that way to be silly. Joe was always being silly. And there was no law against talking to a young girl, or even walking a short distance with her away from her friends, closer to the entrance to a nearby alley. It was all perfectly innocent.

Stanley never mentioned their curious annual ritual or asked his older brother about it–not that year, or any of the subsequent years. There was nothing to ask about really. His big brother was just taking a walk. He was just being silly.

Each year, though, when he noticed the change in Joe's voice about a month before their scheduled pilgrimages, he'd start to tail him, just like he was now. Fairmont was Stanley's turf, Stanley's beat. He wanted to be certain Joe didn't get "silly" closer to home.

There's a box at the top of the hall closet. It's brown and it's square and it's about two-feet deep. There's a thin green pattern of vines around the top, just beneath the lid. When she was younger, Jessica went to it frequently. She hasn't opened it in years. Tonight she does.

When she is sure that her father is sound asleep, she tiptoes from her room and down the hall then reaches up for it. She hurries with it back to her room, closes and locks the door behind her. She sits on her bed and lifts off the cardboard lid.

Three photographs. The first is of her mom back in high school, a bland black and white portrait. The second is of both parents dressed up in a way she doubts they'd ever been again, stiff suit and flowered dress, on their wedding day. Her mom's smile looks forced and her dad's, of course, is barely visible beneath his piercing, serious eyes. The last picture is of Jessica and her mom. It was cut from the *Riverside Reporter*. Jessica was wearing some type of cashier's uniform, work overalls and paper cap, and her mom was pretending to make a purchase from her. The faded caption reads, "Jessica Moon, with her mother, Beverly, at Tenth Street Elementary, learns the value of an honest day's work." Could she really have been that smiling little girl?

There is also a plastic, yellow flower corsage–she's not certain of its origin. There's no sign of it in the wedding picture. Maybe it's from high school dance. She tries to imagine her parents as teenagers, dancing. She can't.

At the bottom, she digs out a chain with two keys on it. She has no idea what they open.

Finally, she lifts out her ragged old one-eyed panda bear, the friend who helped her through many a lonesome childhood night. Inhaling its scent, still familiar after all these years, she remembers how she'd fiddled with the hard, shiny buttons, night after night, and drifted to her dreams. She clutches the doll, lies down and waits for sleep.

Years ago, back in the seventies, the town converged on the fire hall the last Saturday of every month. The same mediocre country band would play, the same smiling couples would dance and sing as the beer kegs emptied and the dance floor filled. Small-town joy.

Joe Senior loved these nights. He loved the way Martha smiled as they danced and the laughter that seemed to fill every conversation. He also loved the spike these dances gave his bar business when afterward, like the pied piper, he was followed by all the grown-ups from the hall to "Joe's Place."

There was one Saturday in January when Joe realized he forgot the blue bank bag that held the change they would need for the night's bustling business. He needed to swing by the house on his way to pick it up. Martha stayed with her sisters, agreeing to meet him at the bar.

On the short drive he smiled as he imagined surprising Joe Junior, then twelve, and little Stanley. They were used to having free reign of the house on dance nights. He'd get a rare glimpse into their freedom.

It's hard to say if his memory is realistic from this point on, or if it's shaped and colored by its years of slavery to this one night. Joe Senior swears (to himself, only to himself) that time slowed down as he parked in the driveway, beside his brother-in-law Kenny's yellow Corvette, and that even as he smiled wondering what the hell Kenny was doing there, he already knew the answer, had already flashed on other Saturdays, on other dance hall absences.

At the exact moment he walked through the house's front door, Kenny emerged from Joe Junior's first-floor bedroom.

"Hey Joe," he yelled, too loudly, with more enthusiasm than the small, quiet living room could hold. "I just stopped by to let little Joe know we were on for the Steelers' game next weekend." The blond-haired golden boy rushed by him, avoiding Joe Senior's eyes and yelling over his left shoulder as the front door slammed. "See you over at the bar."

Joe walked to the door of his older son's room. He stood frozen for a moment, noting the sound of soft Elvis music playing from Stanley's room upstairs. He opened Joe's door barely and peered inside. The sight he saw is exactly as fresh in his mind now as it was then.

His eldest son, his soul, his self, was lying on his stomach with his head buried. Sobs emanated from beneath the pillow. His pants and underwear were like shackles around his ankles.

Joe Senior backed away quietly as he closed the door. Kenny never made it to the bar.

It's part of Chuck Proffer's job as the groundskeeper for Riverside Park to survey his turf once each weekend night to make sure no high school ne'er-do-wells have turned it into Party Central. It's 2:15 a.m. when he gets there. He'd helped to close Joe's, and the eight beers and accompanying shots of whiskey he drank there have him feeling warm and content. The clear summer night doesn't hurt, either. He's always been a happy drunk.

All is quiet.

He sits on one of the benches, overlooking the river, to have a smoke before heading home. It's then that he notices something on the shoreline below. Something shining. The light from the moon is strong enough to help him make out a form connected to the source of the flickering light.

With the grace of a dying moose, he climbs the small fence and angles down the steep dirt hill. His breathing is labored as he awkwardly advances downward. As he nears the shore he realizes that the shimmering object is a silver bracelet and that it's circling a human wrist.

Sobering quickly, he goes to her, kneels, and gently rolls her onto her back. He wipes the mud and dried blood from her face, pushes away her hair, looks with horror at her badly swollen and discolored face. Finally, he realizes what he has discovered: the washed-up body of Tricia Poe. He reaches for his cell phone and calls Joe.

The show went as well as any show can now. Connect the dots. Play the chords. Sing the notes and the words. Smile for the people. The joy has left the music for Finbar, and its absence serves as a constant reminder of the treasure he has lost. He struggles not to feel robbed, not to feel sorry for himself, but as he sings the songs she inspired and which her spirit came to inhabit, the battle is a losing one. He supposes what he's hoping for is the day when the reminders turn joyful again and the music becomes the healing intersection of body and spirit he knows it should be.

He drives home in silence. No radio. No cell phone calls. No windows down. No absent-minded humming. His thoughts turn to Claire. Their friendship has deepened this past week, thanks to her pain, and the timing of their visits.

She's beautiful, he knows. Maybe not in a magazine model way, but in a down-to-her-soul way, for sure. Kind of like Maggie.

Maggie. The tears surprise him, as they always seem to–sneaking up when he least expects them, in a grocery line or on a plane ride. He pulls his car off of I-79 and throws it into park. Here, now, with no need to hide them, the tears flow as freely as they ever do, pouring, the wet flood accompanied by wailing.

He wonders if this is how healing feels.

The apartment is a wreck. It still smells like premenstrual depression. It smells like Tricia. Joe tears off the bed sheets and throws them in the washing machine. As he opens a closet to find their replacement, the phone rings. He picks up the cordless.

"Calm down, Chuck," he says to his panic-stricken friend. "Take it easy, man. Start at the beginning."

"It's Tricia, Joe," Chuck pants. "I'm at the park. I just found her…"

"What do you mean you just found her? She's on her way to California."

"No she's not, Joe. I just found her body here, man. She's dead. I'm really sorry, man. But Tricia is dead."

"Christ," Joe says, his mind flying into troubleshooting mode.

"Should I call the police?" Chuck asks, his voice shaky. "I should probably call the police."

"No," Joe commands. "Just stay with her, man. I'll be right down. Don't call anyone. Don't do anything. Do you understand?"

"Yeah," Chuck answers, ever the servant. "I'll just stay with her."

"Perfect. I'll be there in two minutes."

✦

"Calm down, Chuck."

The words crackle through the unfamiliar darkness. Claire sleeps, but hears them still–Joe Camden's words through the baby monitor. She must be dreaming.

"Take it easy, man. Start at the beginning."

They don't make sense. It must be one of those dreams that don't make any sense. She shifts her position on the comfortable couch.

"What do you mean you just found her? She's on her way to California."

Through the fog of her dreams and her sleep, she wonders if Finbar is back. Maybe she should wake up now, walk back home, sleep in her own bed.

"Christ."

Joe has such a funny voice. He talks like a walrus would talk if it could–all deep and funny.

"No. Just stay with her, man. I'll be right down. Don't call anyone. Don't do anything. Do you understand?"

What is he talking about? Stay with who? Who shouldn't I call? What shouldn't I do? What the hell kind of kooky dream is this?

"Perfect. I'll be there in two minutes."

Perfect. Perfect. Claire murmurs the word and drifts up, tickling the underside of her consciousness. She looks out from her makeshift bed for one groggy moment and stares at the small, white listening device. As sleep returns, she remembers that Will is still in love with her.

146

After talking with Claire, Will kept walking. He bought a coffee at the all-night mini-mart and drank it as he covered the familiar ground. The night is as close to perfect as nights on earth get. The moon is round and full, and the lined streetlights mimic it as he passes. Fairmont. Without cars, without people, it looks like a snapshot of another time. Norman Rockwell's America. Jimmy Stewart's Bedford Falls.

He replays the conversation in his head again now. His brain and stomach churn as he struggles to decipher her tones and her words and the subtle turns of tide. Did she hear what he was saying? Did she start to believe him? Was her weariness at the end a cause for hope or fear? He's tempted to go there right now, throw pebbles at the window, force her up with him. But he knows he needs to respect her every wish through this delicate time.

The good news is he's learned from his mistakes. He's learned that love is worth a hell of a lot more than infatuation. He's learned that while he is capable of being an absolute ass, he is also capable of seeing it, recognizing it, recovering from it. He's learned that Claire Jordan owns his heart and only hopes she won't return it before giving it one more spin.

The caffeine starts to kick in but has the odd effect of exposing his fatigue, not eradicating it. Sleep. Suddenly he realizes just how badly he needs it. How long has it been? It feels like days. It has been days.

At the corner of Allegheny and Fulton he turns right. Up and over, he'll go—back, at last, to his humble abode. As he begins to climb the hill, he turns to watch a car pull onto Fulton, driving quickly away from where he stands, and recognizes it as Joe's. Where is Joe going so late at night? And why is he driving there so fast? A few moments later Will notices Stanley driving in the same direction.

"No rest for the weary," Hank comments to the walls of his apartment. He's pacing. He's going to burn a hole in the carpet. He says that out loud, too. He's tempted to call Irene. They'd only said good night a few hours ago, an awkward handshake in the well-lit bowling alley parking lot, but her perfume still clings to his clothes. They'd stood very close as he helped her form her delivery. Very close, indeed. And she never even considered returning to her group. At least it seemed that way to him.

He resisted the urge to tell her all that was going on with the Moon case. The story was too important to be shared frivolously. And he didn't trust his intentions. But now he rethinks. Maybe she should know what's going on. She'll need to be on standby for when the whole thing breaks.

"It's three in the morning," he yips. "Get a hold of yourself, man!"

Tomorrow is the day. The one toward which his entire life has been leading him. The D-Day of all D-Days. Forget Fairmont, he thinks. This thing could go national. "Larry King, here I come." He practices a pose – a kind of Greg Peck meets Winston Churchill type thing – for the back cover of the best-selling book which will surely ensue, then says out loud again, "Get a hold of yourself, man!"

As he paces and rants, Hank's sleep-deprived mind settles on one of the photographs from the police report, one the police took the day Abraham announced that his wife was missing. They'd looked so plain, those pictures, so utterly devoid of significance. But there it is in the shot of the living room – Jessica's panda bear. The one she couldn't sleep without.

At first Lindsay was okay. She slept even. But then the dream came – the one she couldn't see but felt so hard, it shook her awake. She's not sure what time it is but feels relieved when she hears Will climbing the steps.

Without thinking, she darts from her bed and out the front door.

"Will," she whispers.

He turns and walks back down to her.

"Lindsay," he says with a concern like her mom's, "what are you doing up so late?"

He sits on a step so that they are as tall as each other. His hands on her shoulders remind her of her daddy. She starts to cry. Will pulls her into him. He smells like smoke. He smells like sweat and coffee. But still, she thinks of her daddy, and cries.

"It's okay, it's okay," he says, squeezing her now. "Everything is going to be okay."

Closing her eyes, she wishes so badly that she could believe him.

***

Claire is sleeping. Finbar pulls a blanket from the closet and lays it over her.

"Thanks," she murmurs, not really waking.

"You're welcome," he answers softly.

He stays there longer than he needs to, longer than he should. Makenna cries softly in the bedroom. He warms up a bottle and goes to her.

***

Will watches Lindsay go back into her apartment, understanding more than ever the weight that she carries. He opens his door, stumbles inside, and falls into bed.

His last thought before drifting to sleep is that sadness is a weight we all must carry. Lindsay. Jessica. Claire. Will.

Sadness.

***

Joe doesn't have a plan. He doesn't need one. He knows what has to happen. And he knows it will all be okay. He reaches under the car seat and pulls out his gun, before walking down to meet Chuck Proffer.

8

On that morning twenty years ago, Dominic sat on the edge of the bed. Maria slept peacefully behind him. He couldn't turn to look at her, knowing that one glance would break his heart and his resolve. His decision had been made. He had grown addicted to Beverly's touch. Addicted to the rapture he felt visiting the places she revealed on their stolen mornings together. He wanted, no, he needed to have more.

Dominic stood and dressed. He reached into his bottom drawer for the small bag he'd packed late the night before. Bus tickets. Toiletries. A change of clothes. They'd buy new things when they arrived at their destination, far, far away from the brutal Fairmont winter. They'd find work, start over, and forget everything.

Forget everything.

Summoning every ounce of his dwindling strength, he walked over to Maria. After kissing her forehead he whispered, "I have to get to work early, baby. You stay in bed."

She stirred, smiling through soft, thick layers of sleep.

"Have fun," she murmured.

Unable to speak another word, he turned and hurried from the room.

Several blocks away, the Moon family started its day.

"You take Jessie," Beverly yelled out to Abraham from her stool in front of the bathroom mirror. "The teacher doesn't mind if she's early."

He looked at his daughter. She shrugged, used to her mother pawning her off onto her always-willing father. He helped her on with her heavy white coat then they added the matching gloves and wool hat.

"You're my little snow girl," he said. "Daddy's gonna walk you to school."

They didn't bother calling good-bye. That instinct had evolved out of them through years of no answers. Beverly had adopted her husband's silent stance on life, at least where her family was concerned.

Abraham thought about that as he led Jessica into the cold winter's morning. He thought about how his wife had changed. Early in their marriage, she'd smiled, sometimes at least, laughed even. She'd made fun of his quiet ways, jokingly calling him Abraham Lincoln. What had changed?

By the time he'd delivered Jessica and made it to the Iron Works for his seven-thirty shift, he'd decided that he'd pose that very question to her the next time they talked. Maybe he'd even pick her up some flowers on his way home from work.

Beverly stared at her face in the mirror, searching her eyes for some trace of life. She thought about Dominic and their planned escape. She'd made such plans before but never followed through. This time she would. Come Monday afternoon, they'd be sipping fancy drinks by a pool in Las Vegas.

She'd have to lose Dominic, of course. Though at first she had welcomed his worship and enjoyed corrupting his simple mind, those amusements were fading fast. He was a means to an end. He'd bought the tickets. He'd take care of her for the time being. That was all.

She stood up and removed her robe then studied her full-body profile in the mirror. She'd feared that Jessica had stolen her beauty in the course of the pregnancy but, in fact, the opposite had happened. And her body was as shapely and desirable now as it had ever been. Every day, she felt the eyes of the town's men following her, seeking her out in crowds, behind counters. She liked that power.

In Vegas, she knew, she could put it to good use.

She walked to the bedroom and dressed for work. Her final payday.

Maria's smile disintegrated the moment Dominic left the room. Burying her head in the pillow, she cried and asked herself, "How can this be happening?" They were so happy, she'd thought. Even moments ago, as he'd said goodbye, their closeness felt real, the same. Yet she knew that she was sharing him and had been for months. She'd smelled the other woman's scent on his mail clothes. Mondays and Thursdays.

Her life as a sweet Italian Catholic girl in a sweet Italian Catholic family in which secrets were kept and roles were honored, had taught her how to deal with this. Quietly. It wasn't his fault. He was just a man, and men sometimes did weak things, even when they were strong people like her Dominic was. It had to be the other woman.

Maria vowed to fix the situation.

The buzzing of his cell phone awakens Will early Sunday morning. It's Claire.

"What's up?" he asks, more awake than he should be after such brief slumber.

"I'm worried," she replies. "Something weird happened last night." Will hears her moving. He knows she is pacing. "You know how I told you that sometimes Joe's phone conversations come over Makenna's baby monitor? Well that happened in the middle of the night. I thought I was dreaming, but I'm pretty sure it was real. I think something bad happened, Will."

"What do you mean?"

"Well ... I could only hear Joe's side of the conversation. He was talking with Chuck Proffer, I think, about Tricia."

"She went back to California," Will interrupts. "Joe said they called it quits."

"Yeah, he said that to Chuck, about her going to California, but ... I don't know. There was just something crazy about the whole thing. He told Chuck to just wait there and not call anyone."

"I saw him driving," Will replies. "After you and I talked, I was walking home and saw him driving down Fulton–away from town."

"I think you should call him, Will."

"I'll call you right back."

Will presses the "End" button. The puzzle pieces start connecting as he hits Joe's number on his cell phone speed dial.

"Yeah," Joe croaks.

Will remembers the awkward moment at the bar yesterday when he walked in on Joe and caught him dressing. He thinks of all the times Joe has disappeared into that hidden sanctuary.

"Joe?"

Will sees Tricia's license, remembers her desperate words, recalls Joe's car driving away from him down Fulton.

"Yeah?"

"Is everything okay?"

He remembers a way that Joe had looked at him once. It meant nothing then, but in this new context Will now sees something in it, something resembling hatred.

"Everything's perfect, man. Why do you ask?"

An awkward silence follows.

"Just had a strange dream last night," Will replies. "I'll see you later."

As he hangs up the phone, Will knows three things: everything Tricia Poe had told him was true; something terrible did, in fact, happen last night; and Joe Camden is not at all the man Will thought he was.

✦

Lindsay laces her sneakers. She's so excited. Her mother, whom Lindsay believes is entirely too strict, has agreed to let the young girl go unaccompanied to the outdoor elementary school basketball court across the street. This is a first. Never before has she been given such freedom, and she likes it. A lot.

She considers running upstairs to ask Will to join her but decides against it. She'd prefer that Will just happen to see her shooting all by herself and then join her. She'll shoot there all morning if she has to.

Wearing a smile that covers her whole face, Lindsay grabs the bright orange basketball Will gave her for her birthday and makes for the hoops.

✦

The cancer was supposed to be as vicious as they came. It started in his colon and spread outward, his guts now poisoned beyond hope. He expected pain and was armed with a battery of pills for its arrival. So far it hasn't shown. Not the physical pain, at least. The emotional pain is a different story.

Joe Senior sits on a bench at Vistana and throws feed to the ducks between sips of black coffee. Fountains explode in the middle of the small lake and the elderly couples are out in full force. It's another perfect day in sunny Florida.

He knew that eventually the cycle would end and that the hard memories would take over for good. That's what's happening now. Though he's made it outside, and resisted the urge for more whiskey, his thoughts are stuck on the bad parts.

Idly he contemplates the relationship between demons and sins and marvels at the way each can lead to the other and how sometimes they can even become one in the same. For Kenny, his demon had led to his sin. Kenny's sin became Little Joe's demon and Joe Senior's secret shame, his life's greatest failure, hands down.

For instead of running to his son and lifting him into his giant father's arms, instead of dressing the defenseless boy and driving him to the hospital or the police station, instead of screaming bloody murder and pointing his prominent Fairmont finger at his sick-fuck brother-in-law, he remained silent. Silent. He didn't say a word to anyone, not even to his suffering child.

He drove to the bar that night intending to tell his wife about the monster her brother was, but was struck dumb by her happiness. She was glowing from drink and from the sheer joy of living, and he couldn't bear to dim her brightness in any way. In a single moment, the moment when he should have spoken, he chose the path that led right here—to a dying man in Florida ashamed of the lie he let his life become.

Hank had arrived at the office around seven that morning. Though he tried to keep busy, he mostly just stared at the phone. Finally, just before eleven, it rings.

"Meet me at the old Moon cabin," the disembodied voice instructs. "Be there at one."

Click.

"Document." That's the word that pops into Hank's mind. He runs to the computer to start typing notes. He recounts the progression of events—from the first letter to the last phone call. He wants to have all his facts perfectly straight when the time comes to share them with the world. That time, he knows, will be here soon.

Without even thinking, he once again retrieves the phone from its cradle and calls Irene. He hadn't realized that he had her number memorized. He can't remember ever calling her at home.

"Hello?" her timid voice asks through the line.

"Irene," Hank begins, hoping the familiarity from the night before is still okay. "Hope I didn't wake you."

"It's fine ... Hank."

Why did her using his first name send fireworks shooting through his chest?

"Just wanted you to know that we may be in for some extra work. I can't go into the details just yet, but I think I'll be needing your help to get out a special edition of the paper. Maybe even as early as tonight."

"I'll be waiting by the phone."

More fireworks.

Joe tosses his phone onto the passenger seat. He thinks more clearly when he's driving, which is what he's been doing all night. He knows that he's turned a corner, entered the end game, so to speak. Will knows that Joe was lying. Will knows that Joe has secrets. Joe knows that Will knows. Thanks to Tricia the bitch, Will might even know about Joe's unusual tastes–those fucking movies she found.

He's not worried. In fact, he's happy. It's a beautiful June morning, and today just might be the most exciting day of his life. He throws in *Blood on the Tracks,* another Dylan masterpiece. He'll clean up his mess. He's always been able to clean up his messes. But first he wants to add just a little more to it.

He drives up Pennsylvania Avenue and turns onto Sixth Street. That's when he sees her: Will's little friend, Lindsay, shooting basketball, all by her lonesome on the school playground. Joe loves it when destiny intervenes like this, practically throwing the next move in his face. She's a little younger than he likes them, but still, it's fucking perfect.

The box is still there, tucked at the top of the hall closet where he placed it all those years ago. Abraham pulls it down and digs out the ring with the two keys on it–one for the cabin and one for the gun box.

Returning the container, he remembers Jessica's panda and deduces that she must have removed it at some point over the years. He wonders about Jessica. She stayed in her room most of the day yesterday and is there still. He can't remember her being at home for so many hours in a row since she was a little girl. Maybe she's sick.

He considers knocking and inquiring as to her well-being, but, as always, decides to remain silent.

She hears him outside of her room but knows he won't knock. He never knocks.

She cried all night. It's as if all her life's tears have chosen now to be released–hours and hours and hours of tears.

What is this? Jessica has always relished her control over her emotions. Nothing ever got the better of her. But now she is out of control, crying still as she hears the front door close and her father's heavy boots clomping their steady rhythm away from her.

Her father's steps, away, always away. He'd been doing that, stepping away from her, since the night everything changed. The night she really can't remember at all, if she's being perfectly honest about it. Oddly, though, she remembers the day, specifically, the morning. She can see the way his eyes smiled–the eyes that said more than any words ever could–as he put on her coat. She can smell his skin, feel his hand holding hers tightly as they fought the wind on the way to her school. He'd squeezed her fingers good-bye. That was what he always did, instead of words, instead of a hug or a kiss.

She had loved him more than anything, more than life itself. He was her life. She owns that now as she lies in her childhood bed, her wise, dying Panda Bear observing her as she unravels. She had loved her dad. Admitting that, if only to herself, is new.

⚜

Stanley saw what Joe did last night. He looked down from the Fulton Bridge as his brother shot and killed Chuck Proffer. It felt like TV, like *Columbo* or *Mannix,* the gun firing and Chuck falling over Tricia in the distance like that. Then Joe attached cement blocks to their legs and pushed their bodies into the river.

In all of his years tailing his brother through Fairmont, he never planned out what to do if Joe actually did anything. And Joe has definitely done something. Joe has done a lot of things. Stanley can't hide from that fact any longer.

All night and into the morning Stanley continues to follow Joe's Buick Roadmaster, talking to himself as he debates a course of action. Should he go straight home and call his dad or even the police? He wasn't sure. He didn't want to get Joe into trouble. And he didn't want to let Joe out of his sight either.

Stanley's stomach growls from hunger. He hasn't eaten since dinner last night. He wishes Joe would just go home–so Stanley could think and eat.

Joe's car comes to a stop on Sixth, near Will's place. Stanley notices Will's friend from the T-ball game, Lindsay, shooting baskets on the school court. He stops thinking about his stomach pains, suddenly terrified for the little girl. Seeing his brother emerging from his car, Stanley follows suit. He needs to save Lindsay.

⚜

Claire moves quickly along the sun-dappled sidewalks that lead to Will's and tries to understand the fear she feels. Thoughts of the drama that has transpired between her and Will are gone for now, replaced by a dread she can't quite understand. Neither she nor Will is sure about anything where Joe Camden is concerned. Maybe it's not the emergency they sense.

"Claire, I'm thinking everything Tricia said to me last week was true," Will blurts, the moment she enters his place. The look on his face assures Claire that she is not alone with her doomsday intuition. Will continues, "I think Joe might be a pretty scary guy. There was something cold in his voice this morning that went right through me." Will pauses, then adds, "I just think Tricia wasn't making that stuff up. Deep down, he hates me. Ah, man, Claire–I don't know what the hell to do here."

"We need to find out what happened last night," Claire offers. "What Chuck was calling Joe about. I'm positive it had to do with Tricia."

Claire shares again her foggy memories of the one-sided late-night conversation.

"I have a really bad feeling about all this, Claire."

A scene through the window catches Will's eye.

"Jesus Christ," Will says and runs from the room.

Claire follows.

Lindsay has made three in a row–a new record for her. Taking one step back, she hurls the orange ball. Four.

She sees the scary man with the wolf eyes and the dangling chain running toward her from far across the schoolyard. At the same time, she hears her name called from the opposite direction. It's Will's friend, the funny one, Joe, who always gives her toys. She runs to Joe and away from the scary man.

"It's okay, Lindsay," Joe says as she reaches him. "He's not as mean as he looks, but let's get inside the car just to be on the safe side."

Lindsay is all too happy to comply. She hears the scary man yell for them to stop as she takes Joe's hand and goes with him, faster than she'd expected, practically flying across the playground and onto the street. She is relieved when she hears the doors of Joe's car lock and feels the big safe car pulling away.

"How about if I buy you a Happy Meal before I take you home?" Joe asks, already driving in the wrong direction.

✒

Dominic had always prided himself on being immune to the weather. He never wore gloves, felt they interfered with his sorting and delivering. On that bitter day in January of 1989, though, his hands stuck to the icy wheel and the wind shot right through him as he proceeded with his route. By the time he got to Beverly's the truck was a mess and he was a walking ice cube.

His pulse quickened as he approached the Moon house, even though he knew she would be working. He pondered the fact that the next time he came there would be the last one, and beads of sweat began forming under the folded up portion of his wool postal cap. They'd be leaving on an 8:00 p.m. bus to downtown Pittsburgh. Then a Greyhound would take them clear across the country. Three days. It would take three days to reach their new life. Three days to leave behind all he had ever known.

Could he really go through with this, he wondered? Could he really abandon his wife, his heart, and blaze a reckless new trail? The visceral memory of Beverly's body on his assured him that he could.

Meanwhile, Abraham struggled to concentrate.

"Moon, get your head out of your ass," Mr. Samuels screamed shortly before the noon bell rang. Abraham had caused a back up in the machine assembly line—a first in all his years there. He looked at the older man, nodded, tried to refocus. He'd been thinking about Beverly, about the changes.

Instead of sitting with the other workers in the factory cafeteria when lunchtime came, he grabbed his coat from his locker and left the dank building. He quickly walked the quarter mile to the dry cleaners where Beverly worked. He didn't go in. He didn't want to bother her. He wouldn't even have known what to say, in the middle of the day, in front of Martha and Raylene. He just stood across the street hoping to steal a glimpse of his wife through the window.

Finally, he saw her walking slowly from her seamstress station at the front of the store to the counter. She looked more like a stranger than he cared to admit after ten years of marriage.

Ten years. Where had they gone? And what had become of the woman he'd married? He'd come to accept her temper. It was just part of the deal with Beverly. In order to be allowed the gift of her company, of her presence beside him in their bed each night, he had to accept her outbursts. Patience was simply not one of her attributes. But the cloud around her had grown darker over the past year and created a barrier that he almost couldn't imagine dismantling. Almost.

They said you couldn't teach an old dog new tricks. Well, he'd see about that. He'd buy her those flowers. He'd sit down and talk with her, really talk, the way people did in the movies. He would work hard just like he did all those years ago when he outfoxed Hank. He would take action and get things back to how they were. That was all there was to it. He wasn't sure he could survive losing her. He never wanted to find out.

Miss Robinson was perfect–tall and beautiful. On the morning of January 26, the smiling teacher told her first-grade students to make a drawing of their families.

Jessica Moon spread her big, bright crayons out on the desk. Red, yellow, blue, green, purple, orange, brown, black. She chose red. She started with herself, paying careful attention to the face and hair. Her daddy came next. He was easy. His lines were long and dark and his eyes were big round circles. His was the stick figure closest to hers. Then came her mom.

Miss Robinson walked the aisles, complimenting each child's work. She stared at Jessica's effort and asked, "Where's your mom's face, sweetie?"

Without thinking, the serious girl drew a mean, frowning line, then added a cigarette for good measure.

Hank Shaw had emerged onto the bustling sidewalk with one thing in mind: lunch. Creamed chip beef on toast, to be exact. Pedestrian traffic was surprisingly heavy for such a brisk day.

Hank saw Abraham Moon walking down the opposite side of the street. Hank had trained himself to notice the unusual, and the sight of Abraham walking the street in the middle of the day was definitely unusual. Pretending to window shop, he continued to monitor the quiet man's movements–which stopped across from the dry cleaners.

Hank digested the curious scene. The man who had stolen his love was now stalking her, or at least that's how it looked. Why wouldn't he just go across, walk inside, say hello? How could Abraham have allowed his marriage to come to this, have let that beautiful flower wilt right before his eyes?

The questions triggered a feeling of rage and all of his life's injustices suddenly formed a tidal wave in his chest.

She baked lasagna that Friday afternoon. Whenever Maria was troubled or in pain, she baked. After her mother died. The day they found out that they couldn't have children. Baking was the way she coped. She usually went with cakes, pies or cookies, the sweet scents almost physically easing her burden, but that day it was lasagna–as Dominic worked and his mistress ran free.

Maria knew who it was. Beverly Moon. There was no doubt about it. Two months before, she and Dominic had been out for a walk and happened to spot Beverly in the distance. For some reason, a reason she still couldn't name, Maria had asked her husband, "Who is that woman?"

"Beverly Moon," he'd replied–either too quickly or too slowly, she couldn't recall. In that moment, Maria's fears were confirmed, and the mystery was solved. The other woman was named Beverly. Mondays and Thursdays.

She pulled the tray from the oven then went and got her coat.

Claire and Will reach the schoolyard to find Stanley Camden pacing the basketball court and muttering to himself.

"Where's Lindsay Ramsay?" Will asks. "Did she go with Joe? Where did he take her?" The mentally challenged man continues muttering, clearly agitated, averting his eyes. "Stanley," Will says more sharply. "We need to find Lindsay."

Stanley remains unresponsive, locked in an indiscernible monologue loop.

"What's wrong, Stanley?" Claire asks, softer-toned than Will had been.

"It's Joe," Stanley stammers. "He's gone again."

"What do you mean, Stanley?" Will asks. "Where did Joe go?"

"I tried to stop him. I yelled for them to stop. That girl," Stanley continues. "Lindsay. Joe took her. There's no stopping Joe when he gets like this."

Will's mind races as his eyes lock with Claire's. Looking back at Stanley he asks, "Where would they have gone?"

"I don't know," Stanly replies in eerie monotone. "He doesn't usually do this so close to home."

"Do what, Stanley?" Will yells. "What's Joe going to do?" Will feels physically sick. "We have to find him right now, Stanley. Before Joe can do whatever the hell he does."

"We can go in my car," Stanley says, and the three of them run.

Joe feels like a Duke boy. He almost yells "Yee-Haw" as he zooms up Fulton away from town, his precious cargo tucked safely in the spacious back seat. He pretends to punch numbers into his cell phone then lifts it to his ear.

"Will," he says. "It's Joe. How's it going?"

He pauses, as if to hear an answer.

"Yeah, she's fine, man. We're heading there now."

He pauses again.

"All right. We'll see you there." He tosses the phone down on the passenger seat and yells back to Lindsay, "That was Will, Lin. We're all going to meet in the country for a picnic. Your mom and Will and Claire and everyone. My daddy has a cabin out there. You're going to love it, Lindsay."

"Claire's coming?" the child asks hopefully.

"Yep. Claire's coming," he replies then playfully asks, "Who's up for McDonald's?"

"I am," she yells, smiling so sweetly, so innocently, so ready to believe with those big eyes and that perfectly round face.

Candy from a baby, he thinks as he presses harder on the gas pedal.

9

The mountains are a sea of green. The summer heat has not yet arrived, and the air is still clean and cool up here. Abraham drives with the windows down. Fulton, which starts as a bridge then turns to a hill, leads to this wild, beautiful land. It's amazing to Abraham that more people don't come here more often. It's glorious.

Just past Mile Marker 17, he spots the sign for Camden Lane. The senior Camden loved hunting and had come to believe that his outings could only be successful if he was accompanied by at least one Moon, or both, whenever possible. The three men had spent many a weekend roaming the forest together.

Abraham passes the Camden place now–a nondescript, one-story cabin surrounded by trees and overgrown brush. His family's old place, now also owned by the Camdens, is thirty yards further into the woods. Though the trees make it tricky, it is possible to see one cabin from the other.

He parks on the far side, gets out and opens the trunk in which he had stashed a shovel that morning. As he sets about the task of finding his private marker–a single rose bush he'd planted all those years ago–he thinks through what he is doing, exactly what he has set in motion.

"The truth will set you free," they say, and he aims to test that theory. That's what he is really trying to do–set them free.

The sealed, stainless steel gun box is there, as he knew it would be, ten feet below the ground. He'd even left it loaded.

It takes all of Hank's resolve not to rush right up to the Moon cabin. He knows where it is, of course. Anyone who's lived in Fairmont all his life knows where everything is. The town's landscape and landmarks are bred into the DNA. The Moon cabin, now owned by the Camdens and used for Joe Senior's hunting guests once every few years, is about twenty miles up Fulton Road. Hank had gone there all those years ago, snooped around, hoped for clues. Now the clues, the whole damned mystery, were being handed to him.

Finally the office clock reads 12:15 p.m., the pre-appointed time. Notebook and miniature tape recorder in tow, he walks to his car and heads for the hills. As he drives he can't help noting that life, as he knows it, is about to end. His anonymity, his station as a realtor in a small American town, his modest income–are all about to be blown out of the water. His hands tighten on the steering wheel as he dreams of stardom.

If he owned a cell phone, he'd call Irene.

Claire sits in the back seat of Stanley Camden's car. Will is driving. They've hit the park, the bar and Joe's apartment. As Will and Stanley plot their next move, Claire goes inward. With both windows down and the town's familiar scenery passing, she prays. She really prays. With her eyes closed and her hands pressed together. She'd kneel if there were room.

"Please protect Lindsay," she implores, tears forming on the corners of her closed eyes. "She's such a good kid, God. Please, please, watch over her now."

Stanley's voice breaks through and she hears him say, "He might take her to the cabin."

"What cabin?" Will asks.

"We have a cabin up in the woods," Stanley replies. "My dad used to use it for hunting sometimes ... not so much anymore."

Claire knows instantly with every fiber of her being that Joe has taken Lindsay there.

"Go there now," Claire yells through the wind.

Within moments, Will is speeding up Fulton, and Claire is calling the police.

※

Something isn't right. Joe is being funny and nice just like she remembers, but he's trying too hard. And Lindsay doesn't believe that her mommy would let him drive her far away like this.

"Can I call my mom?" she asks, forcing herself to stare at the passing trees, breathing deeply, the way Will taught her. "My mommy would want to talk to me, I think."

"She's meeting us, Lindsay," Joe insists. "I told you that. Your mom and Will and Claire are all coming to the cabin for a picnic. I'll put on a movie for you until they get there."

Lindsay's heart is racing. As Will's friend turns down the hidden dirt road and they approach the small wooden cabin, she understands that this is the scene from her dream, the nightmare that has kept her up the past week. Only now it's in focus, and she sees what she couldn't before. The person in trouble, the one she'd been wishing she could warn, was her.

※

He knows she is wavering. He sees it in her eyes. He hears it in her soft, trembling voice. She is scared. The child's vulnerability fuels him. He shifts in his seat to allow for his growing erection.

This might be my favorite one of all, he thinks as he puts the car in park, gets out and walks back to open her door.

"Here we are, Lindsay," he announces.

He leads, and she follows. He's always been able to get them to follow. It's his gift, his knack. And always, they realize just a moment too late that they're beyond anyone's help.

The cabin smells like oil and dead animal. There's a wheeled entertainment stand in the corner, and Joe moves it to the center of the room. The TV is the kind that has a VCR in it, and Joe quickly throws in a Disney movie. He vaguely remembers Claire mentioning the fact that she and Lindsay were connoisseurs. As the film temporarily distracts the girl Joe goes back to the car to get the video equipment he always keeps in the trunk.

12:45 p.m. Hank won't be there for another fifteen minutes. If Abraham knows one thing, he knows that the fastidious reporter will not be a moment early or a moment late. That's a given.

He marvels at the state of the firearm he'd just dug up from deep within the earth. Though he'd read that it was possible, he was still surprised at the condition of the gun. It felt brand new, clean and heavy in his hand.

Walking slowly through the woods on what used to be his property, he feels now exactly like he used to feel when hunting with his dad on those crystal winter mornings. His senses are sharper–colors bursting, scents careening, sounds calling. Alive. That's what it is. He is alive again.

What has changed? Sitting on the hollow, dead trunk of a fallen-down oak, he decides that it comes down to ownership. For twenty years he has given ownership of his life and his reputation to Fairmont, and to the memory of Beverly. In deciding to unburden himself of the story that only he can tell, here in the place that holds his childhood, his soul, he has reclaimed his life–plain and simple.

His thoughts are interrupted by the sound of music–loud and misplaced in this natural wonderland. It's coming from the Camden place ... the other Camden place. Funny, he'd driven past it just a half-hour before and not noticed anything or anyone stirring. As he moves closer, he realizes the loud music has been replaced by loud talking. Someone is watching a movie in there.

Instinctively, he knows to keep his presence a secret as he creeps to the lone window on the cabin's back wall. Once there, he crouches, then slowly lifts his head to allow himself a look inside. He scans the room, sees the deer head on the wall, the ancient, aging calendar dangling beneath it, the opened basement door, the TV stand ... and the little girl sitting in middle-of-the room.

Jessica sits smoking on the same Riverside Park bench she and Will occupied less than a week ago. It makes sense to her, she decides, that her dad would have faded, at least for a while. The woman he loved had gone away. He'd needed time to adjust. The problem was, he forgot how to look at her. The eyes, once so kind and expressive, once the perfect audience for every new cartwheel and captured firefly, looked away forever. He still spoke to her, of course; told her how they were going to be okay; asked awkward questions every now and again. But the eyes were gone. And just as his love for her mom had been his foundation, his eyes had been hers.

A switch was tripped, and she fell under her mother's influence even though the damn woman was long gone. Jessica channeled her sadness and disappointment into sharp anger, a steely weapon she used to keep the world at bay. This after Joe Camden had already stolen her innocence.

Finally, here in the blinding sunlight of a perfect afternoon, she sees it all–the tragic unfolding of her own existence. But the tears soften the view, and she begins to feel differently about it all. She begins to feel. With the feeling comes a memory that had been buried deep within her, a memory she was not intending to face, but which she welcomes now. In rushing flashes, she sees that night for the first time in twenty years and knows exactly what became of her long-lost mother.

On that night twenty years ago, Beverly placed a hastily poured bowl of Frosted Flakes on a TV tray in front of Jessica, who watched cartoons in the living room.

"Here's your dinner," she said to the distracted child.

Before returning to the tasks at hand, Beverly allowed herself one lingering look to verify that she felt nothing for her daughter–not anger, not love, not remorse. Nothing.

She returned to the bedroom where she had set out her outfit for the trip: a plain black dress ordered from a catalogue, sheer, black stockings, and black pumps. She knew the bus ride would be long and uncomfortable but still wanted to look nice. Her paisley-print overnight bag held two tops, two pairs of socks and panties, tennis shoes and a pair of blue jeans along with her lone article of lingerie–a black teddy she had owned for five years but never worn. Dominic would buy her new things when they got there; he'd promised.

She brushed her thick, black hair, humming the song that had been playing on the radio when her shift ended and was startled when Abraham entered the bedroom. She was even more startled by the bouquet of roses he held in his hands.

"Who the hell are those for?"

"You," he replied, her sarcasm lost on him. "I want to talk."

"Well I'll be damned," she said to an imaginary audience. "Abraham Lincoln wants to talk. Let me look outside to see if there's any pigs flying."

"Come on, Beverly," he said, "can we please talk?"

"Too fucking late," she barked. "The time for talking is over. I'm getting the hell out of here."

"What are you talking about?" he asked, clutching her wrist, trying to turn her toward him. She broke away and sauntered to the adjoining bathroom.

"Which word didn't you understand?" she asked from the sink. "I'm leaving this shit-hole town and this shit-hole life and going as far away as I possibly can from my shit-hole husband."

"Beverly, get back here," he said loudly. "You can't leave."

"Oh yeah, well just watch me. The man I've been fucking for the past six months is on his way over right now, and we're getting on a bus, and we're never coming back, and there's not a thing you can do about it."

"What about Jessica?" he asked, disbelief swelling in his voice. He joined her in the bathroom and directed his next words to her reflection in the mirror. "You can't just leave your daughter."

"Oh, I think daddy's little girl will be just fine," she shot back and began applying lipstick. "Now let me finish getting ready."

"No," he said, more forcefully than she'd even known he could speak. "You can't leave us. I won't allow it."

"Give me a fucking break," she screamed. "You don't have any say over what I do. And don't think that just because you can suddenly talk everything will change. I gave up on you a long time ago, Abraham. Now get the hell away from me, you pathetic bastard."

The punch landed. Abraham left the room.

Dominic had not gone home after work. He'd braced himself against the January freeze and walked to Duke's instead where he'd eaten a burger and downed three beers and three shots of Jameson. It was not like him to drink for courage, but that was exactly what he'd been doing: drinking for the courage to see their plan through. His hand shook as he lifted the last glass. He settled his tab and entered the frigid January night. She'd be expecting him soon.

Maria's morning good-bye played over and over in his head. "Have fun," she'd said. Walking up to claim his mistress, the whispered words sting with the bitter wind. He'd been having fun, all right—every Monday and Thursday morning. He'd be having fun in Las Vegas come Monday.

Beverly. He struggled to conjure her up, instead of his sleeping wife. He had never seen a woman more beautiful than Beverly Moon. One touch had erased years from his memory. Subsequent touches, the ones that made him blush, then growl, then weep, had obliterated all that remained.

Beverly. Maria. Beverly. Maria. Their names played a tennis match in his head—a psychic metronome marking the time until his rescue. He shoved his hands into his coat pockets and paced on the sidewalk outside of their house.

7:00 p.m. sharp.

Maria couldn't drive. At least she thought she couldn't until she got behind the wheel late that afternoon. She knew where the key went and did better than she could have hoped backing out of their driveway. Her first stop was the post office. She'd parked a block away and watched the staggered string of employees leave. Dominic emerged shortly after five o'clock.

Instead of turning left to walk toward their home, he walked straight across the street and then down the stone steps to Freeport, which he crossed before entering the small corner bar there. Stopping for a drink. That was okay. Men did that.

Too restless to sit and wait there, she'd pulled from her purse the wrinkled sheet of paper upon which she'd scribbled Beverly Moon's address. Operating on blind instinct, Maria drove there, parking close enough to see the front door even in the weakening winter light.

Jessica was used to her mom yelling. It barely even registered. Her dad's raised voice, though, was unusual. Her daddy never yelled. What had her mama done to make her daddy yell?

She listened from her spot on the edge of the sofa as somebody slammed one door then opened another. She heard footsteps descending down stairs. Her daddy must have gone to the basement. What was he doing down there? Why had he yelled? Why was her mama so mean to them both?

She stood and walked down the hallway.

"Daddy," she called tentatively from the top of the stairs. "Are you down there?"

Under any other circumstances she would have stayed where she was. The basement was a place to be avoided at all cost. It was home to, she was sure, many monsters and all the moments from every scary movie rolled into one.

"Daddy," she called out again as she took one, two, three steps down. "Are you okay?"

When she had finally touched every step and stood on the cement basement floor, she didn't see him anywhere. But then she made out his seated outline in the dark corner. It was hard to see but it looked like he was holding something. He was making a noise she had never heard before. Was he laughing? Why would her daddy be laughing? No. He was crying.

"What are you eating?" she asked.

"Jessica," he mumbled, pulling the gun from his mouth, setting it on the workstation shelf, wiping his eyes with the back of his hand. "You better go to your room, little girl."

"Don't cry, daddy," she said. "Everything will be okay."

She held out her small, right hand, and he took it as he stood.

"I know, baby," he said in a thin, soft voice. "I just need to talk to your mama some more."

He walked ahead of her back up the stairs.

Something was happening. With her car still running and the heater on high, she observed the late-day ballet unfolding in the cold, dark world outside. Just before seven Dominic appeared, as she somehow knew he would. And though it pained her looking, seeing him standing, waiting, longing for another woman, she did. Maria looked at him with all the love she had ever felt, willing him toward the right decision, away from Beverly and back to the home where be belonged.

If he chose a different course, if he walked closer instead of farther away, she was prepared for drastic measures. She wasn't sure what they would be exactly. She was just prepared.

Hank worked late that January night. He always did on Fridays. Then he ate at Angelo's. The late work and the restaurant stop were his routine and each led to a culminating ritual. Rain or shine, warm or cold, he walked home the long way this one day of the week just to pass the place he knew she'd be.

That night was different, though. The anger he felt earlier had not abated. It festered and grew. The wind was as loud and menacing as it had been all winter. Branches fell from trees, and the darkness whistled ominous warnings. He shared the night's anger.

As he approached her house, he saw a man stationed on the front sidewalk and slowed his steps to observe. Before he could determine his identity, though, the man walked away. Hank stopped then, too, and stood outside of the Moon house, hoping for a glimpse. He heard raised voices from the unhappy couple within and his anger grew deeper.

Dominic was surprised by the ease with which he changed his mind. He'd made it to Beverly's by the appointed time, even seen her in the living room arguing with Abraham, announcing her plans, he was sure.

And then it hit him like a flash of heavenly light through the earth's darkness. The kind of happiness that Beverly offered was, by its nature, fleeting. It would fade, he was sure of it. But the peace he felt with Maria was enduring. Though it couldn't match the excitement that Beverly offered, it would last his whole life and bring him a truer happiness, the kind of happiness that fills a man's soul with an enduring peace, and that eludes most men. It was the wild rush of the waterfalls versus the gentle ease of the slow, steady stream. He chose the stream, and walked home.

Abraham arrived in the living room to find Beverly pulling her coat from the closet. The sight of her body on display beneath the tight-fitting, black dress and her lips painted red was too much for him. His suicidal despair turned into homicidal rage.

"I'm not letting you go, Beverly," he said evenly, quietly. "If you think you're leaving here tonight, you have another thing coming."

"I am leaving," she replied, her words a taunt, her voice a dagger. "And there's not a damn thing you can do about it."

He moved to her with deceptive speed and grabbed hold of her upper arms.

"Get the hell off of me," she screamed.

"I'm not letting you go," he roared, shaking her body to emphasize each word. "I'm never letting you go."

She yanked herself from his grasp, scratching his arm as she started toward the door. He fisted the fabric of her dress and tugged her backwards.

"You fucker!" she yelled as she spun, lifting a knee to his groin. She grabbed an umbrella from the wall and reared back to swing it at her bent, moaning, pathetic target. Before she could connect, a shot sounded and the fighting couple turned to see Jessica holding her father's gun, pointing it at her mother. The child's trembling hand opened as a confused and wide-eyed Beverly fell dying to the floor.

*

The video camera sits perched atop the tripod, its record light glowing red.

"How's the movie?" Joe asks, standing behind Lindsay, removing his belt and unzipping his jeans. "Huh, Lindsay? Do you like it?"

He walks slowly, savoring these moments when it's all still ahead of him, ahead of them.

"Can I call my mommy now?" the defenseless girl asks as Joe reaches for her and places a hand on the top of her head.

*

"Faster," Will yells as they blaze the tree-lined country. He curses himself for his blindness. How could he have bought Joe's saving-the-world act? How could he not have seen the monster hiding behind Joe's friendly mask? Tricia had even laid it all out for him. How could Will have been so imperceptive?

He wonders if they'll beat the police there. He thinks he hears a siren in the distance.

"It's really close now," Stanley says. Claire and Will move forward in their seats, hoping to aid the car's momentum. Will sees the cabin as they careen down the skinny dirt road. He's out the door before the car even stops.

Three thoughts fill Abraham's mind. The first is of his daughter, Jessica, who had been ten or eleven when Abraham left her with Joe Camden. How many times had Abraham abandoned his sweet, beautiful little girl to this monster?

Then, he thinks of the other little girl, the one sitting in the cabin now, still unaware of the depravity Joe Camden is planning for her at this moment. Abraham wants to traumatize her as little as possible, as he does what must be done.

Finally, he thinks that his whole life has prepared him for this moment. Joe Camden is an animal, and no animal has ever been more deserving of being put down. With his left elbow, Abraham easily knocks out the window then aims his gun and bags his prey.

Hank Shaw is surprised to find two cars parked at the Camden place and to see Will Jameson, Claire Jordan and Stanley Camden running toward the front door. He parks and follows but falls to the ground at the sound of the gunshots.

Will opens the door as he hears the first blast. He instinctively recoils and watches on his knees as Joe falls to the ground like a bag of wet cement. Will leans in cautiously and sees Abraham Moon at the broken window still aiming his gun at the fallen man.

Claire races past Will and rushes to Lindsay.

"It's okay," she murmurs, hugging the girl hard then walking her outside, away from Joe, who writhes on the floor in a pool of red, clutching his leg. "The Little Mermaid" still plays on the TV. "Everything's okay now, Lin," she whispers again and again, wishing she could absorb the girl's fear and sadness with the simple words.

✴

"Get the fuck away from me," Joe screams, though only Stanley has made any move to assist him. Joe's right kneecap is shattered. Blind with rage and pain, he is oblivious to the arrival of the police. "Especially you, pretty boy," he seethes, spit shooting from his mouth like snake venom. Will the writer. Will the stud. Will the fucking bane of his existence. "I shoulda shot you dead a long time ago, you cocky bastard. Let you go talk to Tricia the Bitch for all fucking eternity. I killed her you know? Ever killed anyone Willy Boy? Oh, I forgot, you just write about things. You never do them. Fucking coward."

Yes, this is the way, he thinks. Go out strong. Give your thoughts wings. Let them fly.

"Your daughter was one of my first, old man," he says, noticing Abraham now standing in the doorway beside asshole Will. "She was so fucking tight. What do you think about that? I think I did all those girls just hoping to find another girl as tight as her."

It takes three policemen to restrain Abraham. Three others cross the glass-littered room, one cuffs Joe and the others lift him by his arms.

"You're all a bunch of fucking losers," Joe continues, his consciousness fading now from the loss of blood. "I should have left this fucking town a million years ago. You coming, Stanley?"

Stanley follows behind his handcuffed brother and joins the sad parade as it leaves the cabin.

"I killed 'em all," Joe mutters to no one. "I did 'em, then I killed 'em. How do you like that?"

✴

Abraham, Will and Hank are the only ones remaining. The police took Joe. Claire escorted Lindsay in Stanley's car. Hank has agreed to drive Will. Abraham's car is next door. They'll all need to get to the police station to provide their account of what occurred.

"It was me," Abraham says as the trio lingers. "I was the one who told you to come here, Hank."

Hank and Will stop and turn to face the day's hero.

"It was you?" Hank asks. "Why?"

"I just wanted to get it all out in the open," Abraham explains. "I'm tired of secrets, Hank. I wanted to meet you out here and walk you through everything, everything that happened that night."

"What?" Hank asks, in response to Abraham's obvious reluctance to continue.

Will stands quietly beside them.

"I need you to do me a favor," Abraham finally says.

"Why should I do you a favor?" Hank asks.

"Listen, Hank, I know you won't believe this, but you were lucky I cut in on you with Beverly. I'm sorry for the way that all happened, but I swear you're better off. She would have crushed you.

"Here's the deal," Abraham continues, spurred by Hank's silence. "Beverly was leaving me. She was going to go that night. I tried to stop her. We started fighting."

"What happened, Abraham?" Hank asks.

"Before I tell you, I need you to promise that you won't write about it, or even tell anybody. You have this story, Hank—all that went on here today. Let the other one go."

Abraham can feel Hank wrestling with this demand then finally sees the subtle nod.

"I need more than that, Hank," Abraham says. "Promise me. I need you to say it out loud."

"I promise I won't run the story," Hank answers, finally.

"You too," he says to Will.

"I promise, Mr. Moon," Will agrees.

"It was Jessica."

"Jessica?" Hanks asks. "Your daughter?"

"Jessica," Abraham repeats. "She saw me in the basement earlier that night holding my gun. I was thinking of killing myself. Jessica saw me there, saw where I put the gun. When me and Beverly were fighting Jessica must have went down and gotten it. Beverly was out of control. Jessica killed her mother to protect me." Abraham starts crying, relieved to be sharing this weight that has become a part of him, remembering the things that Joe said, and the agony Jessica must have endured, releasing twenty years of pain and withheld love.

"The panda," Hank says softly. "That's what you wanted me to see. She never went anywhere without it. It was in the police photographs."

Hank rests a hand on the sobbing man's shoulder.

"I don't even think she remembers," Abraham continues, regaining some of his composure. "I don't want her to have to deal with any of this now, especially after what I just found out. I thought it might do us all some good to get it all out, but now I know she's been through enough."

The stillness of the scene is more profound because of the chaos that preceded it. A lone eagle flies high overhead, nearly indiscernible in the vast, white sky. The three men stand together, silent now, bonded forever by this new, shared history.

"The story ends here," Hank says with conviction. "The story ends here."

Joe Senior sits in darkness. Though the night began long ago, he hasn't made a move for a lamp or a light switch. He watches the wall as the same double feature plays over and over. First up, that fateful, horrible Saturday night when he discovered Joe Junior face down on the bed. Next up, the one six days later, the one that plays now.

Martha was asleep. Joe Senior looked in on her and then on both boys. He grabbed his coat from the hall closet. The winter night was cold but clear, the sky a dazzling, brilliant canopy overhead. He checked to be sure that the rifle was on the rack in the truck bed and that it was loaded, then drove out of town.

Kenny lived over the bridge, on a small farm in the no man's land between Fairmont and Sharpsburg. Joe Senior heard whinnying in the stable as he emerged from the truck and reached for his weapon.

With a purposeful stride and without a moment's hesitation, Joe walked to the front door. He knocked and waited as loud steps crossed the wooden floor within. Kenny, wearing a robe over a T-shirt and red sweat pants, seemed almost to be expecting him.

"Hi, Joe," he said. "Come on in."

"Take off your clothes," Joe said, only barely crossing the invisible threshold.

"What are you talking about Joe?" the younger man asked. "Why the hell should I do a thing like that?"

"Take off your fucking clothes," Joe screamed.

Kenny complied. He stood awkwardly, covering himself with both hands as he waited.

"Are you going to kill me, Joe?"

"I'll ask the questions," Joe reprimanded.

The truth was, Joe had no plan. His first thought was to humiliate this man who had permanently humiliated his little boy. After that he supposed he would kill him. But even then, with justice so obvious and so achingly close, he thought of Martha. This was her brother. This was her hero. He changed his course.

"Turn around and bend over," Joe barked, praying the monster would feel even a fraction of the terror Joe Junior must have felt. "How dare you fucking destroy my child's life?"

He spit with the words, his anger an ocean now, a hurricane, tears burning from his eyes, blazing down his cheeks. "How could you fucking do that to your own flesh and blood?"

He wanted to sodomize him then with the barrel of the rifle, violating him in such a way that the evil bastard would feel it in hell for all eternity.

"How many times? How many Saturday nights? How could you do that to my son?"

Joe Senior pulled the trigger on the rifle. A puddle of urine formed instantly at Kenny's bare feet. The bullet left a hole in the ceiling.

"How could you fucking do that to my family?" Joe roared, his need for revenge now like a beast in the room with them. Without thinking, he fired another shot from his rifle, this time hitting a wall lamp. "He's twelve years old, Kenny. Twelve years old."

With this simple statement, Joe's resolve faded into the torment that would accompany him through the rest of his life.

"I'm not going to kill you," he explained wearily. "But if you ever call us, write us a letter, or even think of setting foot within five hundred miles of my family, I'll blow your fucking brains out."

That was the last Joe Senior saw of Kenny Reardon. He never mentioned the incident to anyone. And now he sits alone in his darkened Florida bedroom waiting to die.

Shortly after midnight the telephone rings. The caller ID reveals a Fairmont area code.

10

Abraham returns home by late afternoon. He'd gone to the station house and given his statement. Everyone was in agreement. He had saved the little girl's life. His actions were justified and beyond reproach.

Jessica sits at the kitchen table. It almost looks like she's waiting for him, though he knows that can't be true. She looks up as he enters. Abraham nods hello then walks to the counter to put on coffee.

"Did you hear what happened?" he asks, his back to her.

"No."

"They arrested Joe Camden," he says. "Right after I shot him."

He states this flatly, without animation or emphasis on any word, as if those kinds of things happened every day.

"It's about time," she says in a small tired voice. She wears no makeup and seems to bear no malice today. A welcome change.

He joins her at the square white table they haven't shared in a dozen years. The coffeemaker chokes and mumbles in the background. Though the sun outside is still high and bright, its rays barely reach them there. They sit in near-darkness. He gives her a thumbnail sketch of the day's dark adventure.

"I know what he did to you, Jessie." Abraham fights the tears, but the battle is a losing one, as it had been at the cabin three hours before. "I know what that bastard did."

He's too lost to notice her hand cover his, or the distance her head bridges on its way to his shoulder. He's too lost to think about the fact that she is treating him in a way that she hasn't since she was a little girl–like he is her father and she is his child.

"It's okay, daddy," she says, crying with him now.

"How could I have let him do that do you?"

"How could you have known?"

Back and forth they question and soothe, feeling for the lost world of their connectedness. When the first wave has passed, Jessica makes her confession.

"I remembered," she says, and he knows instantly what she means. He's not surprised. Secrets that are carried off on the wind always return for anyone to see, anyone who wants to, that is.

"You don't need to talk about it if you don't want to, Jess. It's ancient history."

"There's no such thing in this town," she notes. "I think I need to talk."

And talk she does, easily beating her daughter-father word count of the last decade. She tells him every detail that shoots through her head, asking him questions as they arise. He explains how he'd assured her that her mother was going to be okay and then given her a strong sleeping pill, hoping she'd awaken later believing it was all a strange dream. He tells her how he'd systematically brainwashed her in the days following until she believed that her mother had left of her own accord.

Over strong, black coffee, they talk into the night.

"You really loved her, didn't you?" Jessica asks.

"Yeah, I really did."

"Was she ever happy?"

"I think she was only happy when she was sad."

"I relate," Jessica confesses, then tells her father the story of her life.

Officer Dan Conway lets himself into Joe's house. The door is un-locked. Fairmont is the kind of place where you can do that still. At least, it was until this afternoon.

He puts off his search of the premises and sits for a minute in Joe's messy kitchen. The sink is overflowing with dishes. The For-mica tabletop is stained with dried food and dotted with cigarette burns. Dan hadn't known that Joe smoked.

Dan Conway walks the hallway and turns into the first room he reaches, Joe's bedroom. It, too, is a mess. An odor of decay fills the air. The sheets are in a ball on the floor, dirty clothes are strewn everywhere. The room feels like death.

He doesn't know what he's looking for. He was just told to look. He opens each drawer in the dresser and finds a meager assortment of concert T-shirts, underwear and socks, nothing alarming. In the nightstand, he discovers a battered copy of *The Old Man and the Sea,* along with a handless, bandless watch.

He goes through the floor's remaining rooms and finds nothing of note. He notices a cut cord hanging from the ceiling and fol-lows it up to the attic door. When he pulls on it, a wooden ladder emerges, unfolding downward to the floor. He climbs the stairs.

The cold room's single bulb is blown so he relies on his flashlight for illumination. At first scan he sees nothing, just dusty wooden floorboards. But then he notices a square protrusion on the far wall. It looks like it might be some kind of homemade enclosure for household machinery–a furnace perhaps. Reaching it, Dan confirms that it's metal, painted brown to match the wood.

When he pries it from the wall, a brown suitcase falls to the floor. Suddenly filled with dread, Dan kneels and unclasps the rusty latch. His stomach drops when he sees the contents: four hangers–each bearing a different ensemble. One holds a cleric's blacks, another, a policeman's blues. The third holds baggy faded surgical scrubs and a white doctor's coat. The fourth holds what looks to be a security guard's uniform. Joe's disguises. The tools he'd used to lure the unsuspecting young girls.

"Holy shit" he says aloud to no one and rests his forehead against his palms. "Holy shit."

The round earth has turned flat, gravity faltering. Nothing is as it was. Joe Camden is a murderer. His dark, hidden nature means anything is possible, nothing is certain.

Intending to take it into the station as evidence, Dan Conway closes the suitcase. It's then he notices the small gold plate on the front upon which were stenciled two words: *Traveling Clothes.*

Lindsay dreams. Her daddy stands on a beach by the ocean, smiling and waving at her. Her mommy and Phil catch football in the water. She hears them laughing over the sound of the waves. Claire flies a kite in the distance. Will stands watching. Lindsay, even in dreams, has trained herself to expect some terrible calamity, some ominous turn. But as she runs to join Claire, she knows, at last, that no more scary changes are coming. Finally safe, she sleeps until morning.

Joe Senior stands alone outside his son's jail cell. The plane he spent a small fortune chartering had gotten him to Pittsburgh before morning. The sun was only now rising. Joe Junior lies on the cell's single cot, facing away from him.

"Joe," his dad offers. "You awake, son?"

Slight movement. Not a word.

"I'm going to assume you're awake, Joe, and that you can hear me."

Although he's practically whispering, his words sound harsh and brittle in the concrete enclosure.

"Joe, I don't understand what you did … to those girls, to Chuck and to Tricia."

It's difficult speaking with his throat constricting like it is–and dry. He needs water.

"I won't ever understand how you got that lost."

He pauses, seeking the next words, closing his eyes as he shakes his head.

"You ended lives, Joe. You destroyed families. For what?"

He chokes on his question–the words trailing off as he shifts his weight and clutches the cold bars of the jail cell. He forces his gaze up from the ground.

"Joe," he continues, "I need to tell you something. Two things, actually."

The degree of difficulty grows with each sentence. He has the sensation that the air is leaving the space between them, that each word is leading him closer to suffocation. He can hardly continue.

"First, I need to tell you that I know what Uncle Kenny did to you when you were a boy."

He wants to fall, to scream, to exorcise the demon of their shared secret in some way other than this, other than speaking it.

"And I'm sure that one way or the other it made you the way you are. And I'll never forgive myself for knowing that back then and not saying anything–not to you, not to your mother, not to the police or a priest or to anyone."

He suddenly chokes louder than any of his words have been. He breaks down, crying with his head against the steel barricade.

"I guess I thought maybe you'd be embarrassed if I brought it up. Or maybe I just couldn't face it myself. I don't know, Joe. I'm so sorry."

He's convulsing now, lost to it, whatever it is. He wishes that tears could wash away time and take them back to before Uncle Kenny, before Joe's killing spree. He forces himself forward, needing to say all that he came to say.

"But that still doesn't excuse what you became, Joe, what you did. Lots of people have bad stuff like that happen to them, Joe, and it doesn't turn them into monsters. Do you know what you've done?"

He's yelling now, pleading, for what, he doesn't know. Recognition? Mutual repentance? The form on the bed remains still, save for the breathing. No words of reply are offered. The shuddering wave of awareness passes. Joe Senior continues, "The other thing I wanted to tell you, Joe, is that I love you."

This is an afterthought, a small token against the mountain of their mistakes. His words are like sand, like dirt, like nothing.

"No matter what you did, I love you. And I forgive you."

He's barely audible now. Speaking to himself as much as to his boy.

"I doubt many others will, but I do."

Slowly, Joe Senior walks away from his namesake.

Hank and Irene race the clock to get the special edition out by morning. Information trickles in from around the country, though the full extent of the carnage left by Joe Camden won't be fully revealed for weeks, if ever. A pattern is emerging, though.

Unbeknownst to the world at large, Joe's famous "musical sojourns" in which he'd travel with his brother to faraway cities each year for this benefit concert or that favorite artist, were always accompanied by an "episode." Dressed as a policeman, a priest, a doctor or a security guard, he would win the trust of an unsuspecting young girl before making her his victim. He'd taken fifteen such trips over the past fifteen years.

Also, at the urging of Stanley Camden, the police dragged the river and found the bodies of Tricia Poe and Chuck Proffer–two more to add to the death toll.

How? How could none of us have seen this? How could we not have known the evil that was lurking in our midst? These are the questions Hank keeps asking himself. They're the questions the whole town will be asking by morning.

As Hank and Irene work, they touch. At first the touching is purely incidental: a brush of hands as they both reach for something, a glancing of arms as they pass each other in the small office. But gradually the touching becomes intentional. As each piece of the tragic, twisted puzzle falls into place, a need fills the room around them, their need for one another.

Before running to the printer with what Hank hopes is a clear and professional telling of all that has occurred (along with some patented Hank Shaw expert analysis thrown in for good measure) he turns to the woman he has worked with and admired for so many years.

They kiss with a hunger that neither of them knew they possessed. It had been their burden for years but disappears in an instant. Aside from his mother, Irene Turtleman is the first woman Hank Shaw has ever kissed.

Stanley watches *Columbo*. It's his favorite episode – the one with the famous country singer, Johnny Cash. The faces of the girls keep appearing in his head. He forces them away, talking loudly with the befuddled screen detective.

He had trained himself not to think about the girls, not even to consider the possibility that Joe might be doing anything improper after Stanley turned away. He had blocked all of that out, aided by the fact that Joe seemed so normal, so happy, the following mornings. But now Stanley remembers each of their smiling faces.

He told the police everything. He started with Lorena and went down the list. He was surprised by how much he remembered – the thick glasses a little girl in Boston had worn, the sad, downcast eyes of the one in Tennessee, the way Joe acted perfectly fine afterwards as he mapped out the last day of their vacation.

As he talked, Stanley began to realize how stupid he'd been to look away and that he could have protected those girls, and Chuck Proffer and Tricia. Hearing Joe screaming at everybody, watching the monster emerging like that in front of everyone, made Stanley see what an idiot he was for not letting himself see the truth.

Good cop, bad cop. Stanley had been the bad cop. He had turned a blind eye. He had accepted the bribe of his brother's love in exchange for a killer's freedom. He was definitely the bad cop.

He tries to force his concentration back to the television but can't quite manage it. A familiar voice cuts the battle short.

"Stanley," his father yells from outside. "Stanley, are you in there?"

Stanley stands and rushes to the door, to his dad. The grown men embrace, each one's tears seeming to draw out the others'.

"I let him do it," Stanley blurts. "I could have stopped him, daddy, but I didn't. I should have stopped him."

Joe Senior pushes Stanley away, holds his son's arms in such a way that eye contact is unavoidable. His father's eyes look so sad, so heavy. And he's thinner than the last time. His dad looks old.

"It shouldn't have fallen on you to watch over your brother like that, Stanley. That was my job. I'm the one who screwed up. Not you. Look at me, buddy. Are you hearing what I'm saying?"

Stanley nods.

"Joe took advantage of you. It wasn't your fault. It had nothing to do with you."

Stanley nods more convincingly now, beginning to understand and believe, happy to be safe with his father again. The two men sit quietly together and watch the rest of *Columbo*.

Early Tuesday morning Claire packs her suitcase. The town is still reeling. News trucks line the streets. And though the catalyst was tragedy, Fairmont is drunk on its celebrity. Claire can't wait to leave. Finbar and Makenna are due to pick her up in twenty minutes. She'll be singing for two thousand people in Columbus, Ohio, that very evening.

Will stirs in the bed and opens his eyes. Though he's stayed with Claire the past two nights, the distance between them has not diminished. In fact, it's grown wider. They talked for hours about Joe and Abraham but when it came to their own situation they had surprisingly little say to one another.

Claire has been up for hours trying to understand what has happened, what she is feeling. As Will lifts himself into a seated position she presents her conclusions.

"Will, I had just gone through a major ordeal. I was as sad and vulnerable as I've ever been in my whole life. I trusted you to love me and to be with me, if not in body, at least in spirit. You disappeared.

"I don't think you're a bad person, Will. In fact, I really love about ninety percent of you. It's that other ten that I just can't live with. And I have a feeling it will always be there."

Before he can respond she raises her arm and says, "I don't want to talk about it. I just know this is good-bye."

She'd expected to feel more overwhelmed by the emotions surrounding this speech but is calm and collected. She picks up her guitar and her suitcase.

"Good-bye," she says. "Lock the door when you leave."

Jessica sits on the ground beside her mother's unmarked grave.

"I know why you hated me," she says. "You hated me because he loved me." She draws a line in the dirt with her finger. "What you didn't understand, though, was that he loved me because I came from you. Why couldn't you have just let him love us both? Why couldn't we just have shared him?"

A breeze manages to find her through the thick trees. Jessica shivers in the shade.

"I'm sorry for what I did to you, mama," she says. "I didn't know what I was doing. I just didn't want you to hurt him anymore."

A lone tear draws a clear, thin line down her cheek, but it is the only one. None follows. None will—at least, not now.

"Good-bye," she whispers and stands to reenter the world.

✳

Bartholomew Tucker explains the Buddhist notion of life as suffering to an uninterested bartender. Dominic sits at the bar of "Duke's," the place Joe's regulars have already adopted as their new home. Larry is here, Bartholomew, even Hank Shaw and Irene. The surprise guest today, though, is Abraham Moon, who enters shortly after five and sits beside Dominic.

"I'll get this round," Dominic says as Abraham orders a whiskey and soda.

"Thanks," Abraham grunts. The surrounding chatter resumes as the two men drink. After several sips Abraham says, "I saw you."

"Pardon me, Abraham?" Dominic asks.

"I saw you."

"You saw me where, Abraham?"

"I saw you outside of our house that night, waiting for her on the sidewalk. I saw you."

Dominic doesn't respond. He doesn't know how to respond.

"It's okay," Abraham says. "I know what she did to people. I understand."

Dominic can't explain the tear that forms in his eye. He thinks it might have something to do with his wife. With Abraham's forgiveness, comes Maria's. He doesn't know why. He doesn't know how. But he knows.

✳

There are two signs posted on the door of "Joe's Place." One reads, "Closed" and the other reads, "For Sale." Joe's dad had swept into town and closed the bar after offering public and private apologies. He was beyond sorry for his eldest son's unspeakable, unforgivable deeds. He hoped and prayed the families of the victims could find peace.

As a final gesture of remorse, the broken-hearted old man gave Will and Donna some money to "make a new start." It was more than Will needed to live for a year. The time to write his first novel has clearly arrived.

To that end, Will sits at his desk Thursday afternoon and tries to get his creative juices flowing. Nothing comes. He feels too restless. He stands and paces the creaky wooden floor. He throws a tennis ball against his wall for a short-lived game of catch. He gathers up his dirty clothes.

At one point he starts packing his duffel bag thinking, "Screw it, I'm going after Claire." But his resolve fades as he realizes she was right, he's not ready, he would surely let her down again. He's almost relieved that she is gone.

At that moment he realizes something. He wants to talk to Jessica Moon. When he looks over the past week, she's the one who shines through best and not just because of her crazy beauty. There is something deeper there, something he wasn't expecting to find. He grimaces as he remembers his last words to her. "You're just so beautiful." Jesus. How patronizing could he be?

And now he understands her better. He knows that not only is her bark worse than her bite, it stems from a sadness that had been foisted upon her by her mom, and later, by Joe Camden–a sadness of which she was a victim, not a creator. She becomes even more beautiful in his mind's eye.

As the outdoor late-day sunlight weakens and fades, he picks up the phone. Feigning courage not even close to being real, he calls "Information" to ask for the number and lets the helpful operator connect him directly. After seven rings he hears her voice's "Hello."

"Jessica, it's Will," he says. "Please don't hang up."

She doesn't.

✹

Dan Finbar sits in the breakfast room of the Columbus Marriott. He hasn't slept all night. After a show that went better than he could have hoped (including Claire Jordan's well-received opening set), Fin and Claire had talked into the early hours of the morning, first basking in the energy of the gig and then going over all the details Claire knew of the Joe Camden and Beverly Moon stories. Will had given Claire the inside scoop in their last day together and Claire shared it all with her new employer as his baby slept peacefully in the Pack'n'Play. Finbar's mind is still buzzing from it all.

His new MacBook is opened on the table in front of him, right beside his barely touched bowl of Raisin Bran. His hands are poised atop the keyboard.

He's written songs his whole life, practically. Songwriting has become second nature to him, maybe even first nature, above the speaking involved in normal human interactions. And yet, writing his long, sad suicide note up in Pembroke, the "note" he is so grateful to be alive to share most mornings with his beautiful daughter, the note detailing his friendship with Ransom Seaborn and his love affair with Maggie Stuard, has made him realize something: he likes writing long-form. Songs are so short, so finite, and you have to express all your thoughts, paint the whole picture, in three or four minutes. But with a book, a novel, he could take as long as he needed.

An elderly couple takes the table next to his. The woman, short, with dyed red hair, sits as the man, even shorter and with no hair at all, sets about the complicated task of preparing waffles for the two of them. He calls over to his wife, asking if she wants coffee. Finbar smiles.

He feels better than he's felt since before Maggie died. A song awakened him two days ago, the unclaimed, as-yet-unwritten kind. For the first time in nearly a year he picked up his guitar and began chasing it down. He didn't find it all, but he will.

The tour bus leaves at noon then they drive five hours to Chicago. Finbar will sleep then. Right now he just wants to write, not a song, not a poem, a novel. He wants to write more words than could ever be forced onto a piece of music. He wants to create a world and live there for a while, see what it shows to him. He wants to tell a hard, sad story.

He finishes his cup of coffee and returns his gaze to the empty word document on the screen. With a deep breath and steady hands he begins.

"Beverly Moon walks slowly along Allegheny Avenue..."

Bill Deasy is an accomplished songwriter and recording artist.

When he's not traveling the globe in support of his music,
he lives with his wife and kids in Oakmont, Pennsylvania.

Special thanks to my readers, Dana Allwein and Bill Deasy; my "research assist-ant," Stephen DiGioia; and my long-ago sounding board, Dave Brown.

Thanks also to Holly Elspeth Ollivander for believing always and again, and to Huw Thomas and everyone at Velluminous Press for strapping on the skates and taking another spin.

Breinigsville, PA USA
04 November 2009
227009BV00001B/56/P